R2 STOCKPORT

BED OF NAILS

Following a personal tragedy, Chris Randall travels around the country in his Dormobile, not caring which hospital employs him next as a locum laboratory worker. He is looking forward to working again in Oxford because of his friendship with John Devlin, who is working in secret on a cure for AIDS. When he arrives, John is missing and the more he tries to find out, the more hostile John's erstwhile colleagues become. Attempts are made to make Chris leave Oxford, but with the help of John's ex-girlfriend Sally he tries to solve the mystery. Then he is arrested for murder...

BED OF NAILS

BED OF NAILS

by

Andrew Puckett

Dales Large Print Books
Long Preston, North Yorkshire,
BD23 4ND, England.

British Library Cataloguing in Publication Data.

Puckett, Andrew
    Bed of nails.

    A catalogue record of this book is
    available from the British Library

    ISBN   978-1-84262-707-5 pbk

First published in Great Britain in 1989 by
William Collins Sons & Co. Ltd.

Copyright © Andrew Puckett 1989

Cover illustration © Dave Wall by arrangement with
Arcangel Images

The moral right of the author has been asserted

Published in Large Print 2009 by arrangement with
Andrew Puckett, care of Dorian Literary Agency

Dales Large Print is an imprint of Library Magna Books Ltd.

Printed and bound in Great Britain by
T.J. (International) Ltd., Cornwall, PL28 8RW

Acknowledgments

My wife, Carol,
for constant encouragement

My mother, Pamela Puckett,
for typing and advice

For my friend, David Huntly
1949-87

CHAPTER 1

The Dreaming Spires rose up from the city as I came down from the Swindon road, pricking the skyline like the spears of a waiting enemy, like a set of surgical steel lancets...

No, I'm wrong. You can't blame a city for your misfortunes and even if you could, Oxford hadn't done anything to harm me, not then. I was looking forward to working there again, to seeing John and Sally, and hadn't the faintest notion of what lay in store for me as I start – stop – started along the Monday-morning traffic jam.

How could I have known that within a week I would be charged with murder?

I left Bile (my bilious green Dormobile) in the hospital staff car park and hurried over to the old Georgian block. It looked better in May than it had last winter, the stonework glowed and I could see the water from the fountain at the front of the building glittering in the morning sun.

The laboratory was in a side wing, and as I approached, a car pulled up in front of the entrance and a familiar athletic figure with crisp dark hair climbed out.

'Hello, Charles,' I called. 'Not escaped yet?'

His face froze for a moment when he saw me, then relaxed into a smile as he came forward with outstretched hand.

'Sorry, Chris, didn't recognize you at first. Yes, I'm still here,' he said as we shook hands. 'The firm keeps bringing out new products, and this lab is the ideal testing ground. Besides which, I like it here.'

'Oh yes, I'd forgotten. Oxford's your home from home, isn't it?'

He smiled. 'Actually, I *am* escaping, as from tomorrow. I've got a week's leave.'

'Going anywhere?'

'Greece.'

'Lucky chap. I envy you.'

He looked at me curiously. 'What brings you back, Chris?'

'Oh, apparently they're short-staffed again, so they've sent for me, via the agency.' I made a mock bow. 'At your service, sir. Anyway,' I said as I saw Carey's Range-Rover approaching, 'I'm a bit late, so I'd better get on.'

'We'll have a drink some time,' he called

after me as I was swallowed by the gloom of two flights of dingy stairs.

The clock in Reception said 9.20, I *was* late; they were all in, and all looked round at me as I pushed open the door of the main laboratory.

Sally's face showed as much surprise as the others, but at least hers was tinged with pleasure.

'Chris! What are you doing here?'

'Working, I hope. The agency said you needed someone.'

'Yes, but … we didn't think…' She turned to Philip Snow, the section head in that area. He was already coming towards me.

'There must be some mistake, Chris,' he said in a low voice. 'We were told it wouldn't be you.'

'Oh. Does it matter?'

'Not as far as I'm concerned, but… Look, you'd better wait here while I tell Ron.' He made for the door.

The others, about ten of them, turned back to their benches and resumed working as I walked over to Sally.

'What was that all about?'

She shrugged helplessly. 'Ron said only last week that you weren't coming back – he seemed so certain about it…'

15

'Never mind,' I said. 'How's things?'

She made a mouth. 'You know John and I have split up, I suppose?'

'He told me when he wrote a couple of weeks back. I'm sorry.'

'Don't be. I only wish it had happened months ago.'

'When did it happen?'

'Just over a month–' She broke off as Ron and Phil came back.

'I'm sorry, Chris,' said Ron in his strident Yorkshire as he came towards me. 'It won't do. You can't stay here.'

'But you have asked for a locum, haven't you?'

'I asked for a virologist, we need someone who can culture cells.'

This was news to me. 'Well, I've done some cell culture…'

He was shaking his head. 'It has to be recent, Chris, not a week ten years ago when you were at college.'

'I've just had a month in the Virology Unit in Birmingham,' I said mildly, 'culturing cells. I wouldn't have thought your methods would be that much different here.'

It was pure luck. Before Birmingham, my knowledge had been pretty much as he'd described.

I looked at him curiously. Behind his spectacles, his eyes were hunting around and you could feel the rest of the room tuning into us.

'All right,' he said at last, 'a week's trial. But I'm warning you–' he held up a pudgy finger – 'if I find someone more suitable in the meantime, I'm taking them on. Show him where to go, Phil.' He strode out.

I turned to Phil in amazement. 'What on earth's got into him?'

He shrugged his lean shoulders. 'You know what he's like when he's got a bee in his bonnet about someone. Come on, I'll take you to the cell lab. You'll be working with Ian Lambourne.'

I turned to Sally. 'See you later. How about lunch?'

She smiled and nodded and then I followed Phil into the corridor.

As we reached the Research Unit where John worked, I said, 'Excuse me a moment,' and put my head round the door. John wasn't there.

'Where is he?' I asked.

Phil said quickly, 'Don't ask me.' And then, 'He'll be in later, I expect. You know how he pleases himself.'

Ian and I remembered each other and the

work held no surprises, so we settled down quite easily. Unlike bacteria, which can grow almost anywhere, viruses need live mammalian cells in which to grow, so to culture them you have to culture the cells in glass test-tubes first. It's tricky, but rather tedious work.

We reached a natural break at around 10.30 and went along to the rest-room. Heads lined the walls, mostly bent over books or magazines, but John's sandy hair wasn't among them. I helped myself to coffee and sat down.

Silence reigned, as usual.

Most of the faces were familiar or half-familiar, but there were one or two new ones, I noticed.

'Anyone heard anything from John yet?' I asked.

Ron spoke. 'We've learned not to expect that kind of courtesy from *Mister* Devlin.'

Silence reigned again. I should have remembered, no one liked to speak while Ron was still in the room...

A pair of eyes that had flickered up when I'd mentioned John's name remained fastened to me. He was sitting in the corner, a keen-featured man with neat brown hair. He didn't look away when I glanced at him, but continued to regard me thoughtfully.

'Well, Ron's certainly got it in for you,' said Sally an hour or so later over her pie and chips. No slimmer, Sally.

'So what's new?' I said gloomily.

Sally didn't need to be a slimmer. She had one of those big, gorgeous figures that can take spare flesh. She also had milky skin and wide grey eyes framed with long gold hair.

'No, I mean it,' she said, 'I overheard him 'phoning your agency. D'you know what he said?'

'No, but I expect you're going to tell me.'

She leaned forward. 'He was furious with them, called them all sorts of names because they thought he'd asked especially *for* you, when in fact he'd said he'd take anyone *except* you.'

I sat up. 'Really?'

'Really! He demanded they send someone else immediately, but I gathered they didn't have anyone. Anyway, I had to move after that because Dr Carey came into the corridor.'

I said slowly, 'I know we didn't get on, but … saying he'd take any locum except me … don't you think that's going a bit far?'

She shrugged. 'Who can explain the workings of Ron's mind?' Then, after a pause: 'I think, in his mind, he'll always associate you with John, and you know how he feels about John.'

'Perhaps you're right.' I looked up. 'You've no idea where John is, have you?' She shook her head. 'I think I'll look round after work in case he's at home.'

'Give him all our love if he is.'

'Bitch,' I said, grinning. Then: 'Sally, who's that new bloke, the smallish one who was in the corner of the rest-room? I've not seen him before, have I?'

'Oh, that's Dave, he's been seconded to us to look at our data-handling system. He came last week, I think, or was it the week before?' She looked up. 'Why?'

'No reason. Why don't you and I go out tonight for a drink?' I said it impulsively, forgetting about John for a moment because she looked so good.

'I'd love to, but I can't.'

'New boyfriend?'

She smiled coquettishly. 'It depends.'

'Depends on what?'

'What happens tonight.' She grinned. 'Tell you what! You can take me out tomorrow and I'll tell you about it.'

Shortly after this, we went back to the lab.

20

She's got her confidence back since leaving John, I thought. Certainly hasn't taken her long to find a new beau.

The afternoon passed quickly enough and at five-fifteen I was on my way round to John's flat. He lived in the rabbit-warren of terraces in the triangle between the Iffley and Cowley Roads, the sort of area that used to be looked down on, but to which the estate agents are now awarding 'Character', because it's more than seventy years old.

Up two flights of dim lino-covered stairs in a nameless street, to a small landing; I knocked on the dark varnished door.

No answer.

I knocked again and said softly, 'John, it's me, Chris.'

Silence.

I tried the smooth brass handle, but it was locked.

'John, are you all right? Come on, I won't give you away.'

The door on the other side landing opened and I turned to see a grey, unshaven face peering like an animal out of its burrow.

'He ain't there.'

'D'you know where he is?'

The face seemed to retreat as I approached. 'No.'

I thought quickly. 'When was he last in?'

'Dunno. Friday, I fink.'

'Did he say he was going away?'

'No.' The door began to close.

'Wait a minute – is there anyone he might have left a message with?'

'Dunno. Landlord mebbe.'

'Where can I find him?'

'Next door. Number free.' He disappeared as the door clicked shut.

I thoughtfully descended the stairs and found number 'free', the next house, wondering why it is that so many natives of Oxford seem unable to pronounce 'th'. I knocked.

Again.

Not in, or just not answering, it could be either round here.

I climbed back into Bile and wound down the window. Then pulled out John's note.

Dear Chris (it read),

Thanks for your letter. It'll be good to see you again, too, except that you'll have to see me and Sally separately now. Well, I knew it would happen.

I'm nearly there, Chris, just one more heave! If the bastards'll give me a little peace, the whole project should be finished by the time you're here. America, here we come! I've had one offer already, but I'm hanging on for a better one. We'll go out Monday night and celebrate and I'll tell you all about it.

John

Not the letter of someone who's about to do a bunk, I thought as I put it away. So where was he?

I drove Bile over to the small car park I'd found last year, sandwiched between the canal and Port Meadow. Beside it was a small piece of waste ground surrounded by willows where I wouldn't be in anyone's way. I cooked a meal and slowly ate it before having a wash.

Then I listened to the radio for a while without paying very much attention, as I stared across the broad sunlit expanse of the meadow. The truth was that I didn't know what to do with myself. Walk across to the Perch for a drink, perhaps? No, for once I wanted someone to talk to.

Then I remembered Charles's suggestion that morning that we have a drink, so I quickly tidied everything away and drove over to where he lodged when he was in Oxford.

His eyes widened in surprise as he opened

23

the door. 'Hello, Chris. What can I do for you?'

'You can let me buy you that drink you mentioned this morning.'

'I'm in the middle of packing just at the moment.' A tiny wave of irritation crossed his face before his customary good manners reasserted themselves. 'Come on in a moment, I won't be long.'

I followed him to his room where a case lay open on the bed.

'Actually, I've nearly finished. Sit down over there while I check.'

I sank into a comfortable armchair while he muttered to himself as he went through the contents of his case.

'That'll have to do,' he said, snapping it shut. 'I'll come out and have a quick one with you in the local, then I really must go. Got to be up by five tomorrow.'

His local was just that – about four doors away. I bought a couple of pints of bitter and took them over to where he was sitting.

'Charles, I'm sorry if I came at a bad moment, I should have realized you'd be packing.'

'That's all right, it was my suggestion. I'm rather glad you came now. Cheers.' He took a mouthful of beer. 'Although I can't think what I've done to deserve this honour. I'd have thought you'd have been out with John.'

'He's not around. He wasn't at the lab today, didn't you know?'

'I hadn't noticed, but then our paths don't tend to cross much.'

'No, I suppose not.' I drank some beer myself. 'Nobody seems to know where he is.'

'He'll turn up. Like the bad penny he is.' His voice trembled slightly and I looked up. He compressed his lips in a small gesture of resignation. 'I'll be honest, Chris, I've never understood how you two got on.'

'Just one of those things.' I had no intention of trying to explain to Charles something I didn't really understand myself. 'Tuesday seems an odd day to start a holiday,' I said to change the subject.

'It was a cheap last-minute offer. There's a lull in my work at the moment, so I grabbed it.'

'Don't blame you,' I said, a trifle wistfully. 'What *are* you doing in the lab at the moment?'

His face lit up. 'A field trial of our new HIV antigen test. If it works the way we think it does, it'll revolutionize HIV serology.'

I listened with half an ear while he delved into the minutiæ of the test and was almost relieved when he said he must be going. He had to go to his flat in London to collect his passport.

I drove back to the trees. It was only 9.0 and the sun hadn't yet gone down. I tried to read a book but couldn't settle to it. My mind was restless with thoughts and my heart seemed filled with anxieties and emotions I couldn't place.

Impatiently, I locked up Bile and set out across the Meadow to the river. Stood gazing at the reflection of the poplars in the water while their leaf music washed over me. Upstream, the surface of the river glinted like a ribbon of mercury in the evening light.

I turned and walked downstream to the bridge, then up past the boatyards on the other bank to the Perch, where I sat drinking in the garden, trying to sort out my thoughts and feelings as the swallows shrilled overhead.

As the light faded and the bats flitted silently to and fro, such a feeling of unreality took me for a moment that I had to grip my legs to make sure they were really there.

One year ago I would have been sitting like this in Somerset with Jill. Suddenly then – and now – were a thousand years apart, yet separated by only a paper-thin sheet of glass...

Glad of the darkness, I buried my face in my hands.

They say it's best when death comes quickly. I don't know. They say that the words that you last spoke together aren't important. I hope not.

We'd quarrelled and she'd stormed out of the house. I'd heard the car accelerate furiously away. I didn't begin to worry until nearly two hours later, by which time she'd been dead for over an hour.

They tell me she didn't suffer and sometimes I believe it, but not a minute passes when I wouldn't give my life to be able to say 'sorry'.

I've heard it said that luck evens itself out over a lifetime, and I suppose my own life had been pretty cushy until then. Except, perhaps, when my parents died.

I'd inherited their house in Watchport and had lived there ever since. With no money problems and no other worries, I'd drifted through a life that was maybe a little dull, until Jill had come along and given it the seasoning it needed.

After she was killed I had, well, medical problems and didn't go back to work for nearly two months. When I did, they were all terribly sympathetic. Terribly.

I am – was, rather – a Senior Scientific Officer in a hospital laboratory. I'm good at my job, I like it, but I knew by lunch-time that I couldn't stay.

So I signed on with Athena, a London-based agency that handles locum lab workers; bought and equipped Bile and a month later was on the road. Athena have London pretty well covered, so I go anywhere else, Birmingham, Cardiff, Reading, for however long I'm needed. There's plenty of work. Medical laboratory staff are leaving the profession in droves as the pay and prospects grow worse, and Athena are always having to answer cries for help.

I'm a nomad, but only a semi-nomad, since I usually go home to Watchport for weekends. I like the life. It's a good way of keeping people at arm's length, of being alone when I want to be alone.

I walked back unsteadily across the Meadow in the moonlight, drank some water and fell into bed.

But not to sleep. The leaves of the willows outside seemed to carry a message different from the poplars, so I listened, and thought about John and Sally and how we'd met.

It was certainly different when I'd started locum work, autumn, and getting colder every day. I soon learned how to wrap up warmly though, and to use the shower and canteen at whatever hospital I found myself. Jan. and Feb. were no joke, mind you, and I took hospital accommodation when I could and damn the expense.

Anyway, the job at the National Microbiology Laboratory in Oxford was my third and I had been looking forward to working somewhere civilized for a change – that's a laugh!

It was mid-November, I had arrived early at the lab and Sally was the first person I saw, a flash of gold by the window as she'd turned her head.

'Oh, hello,' she'd said, 'you must be the new locum. I'm Sally.'

'Chris.' I held out my hand.

She turned back to the window. 'Look at that. Magic. I never get tired of it.'

Outside, the sun was rising through the mist over the line of the rooftops. The Dreaming Spires, scattered like chess pieces, seemed to repel the surrounding opalescence with their solidity and yet to belong to it at the same time.

'It's beautiful,' I murmured. And then after a pause: 'I don't think I'd ever get tired of a view like that, either.' I turned to her with a smile. 'Do you know what they're all called?'

'Oh yes. You see that one, trying to look like St Paul's, that's the Radcliffe Camera. And over there, rather aloof, is Tom Tower, and next to it, this hospital's namesake, St Frideswide's. Or should that be the other way round, the hospital the Cathedral's namesake?'

Sally had this wonderful gift of being able to put anyone at ease and soon we were talking like old friends. She asked me where I was staying and I rather self-consciously told her about Bile.

'So you're a sort of gipsy,' she said, looking at me with new interest.

'Left the earrings at home today,' I said apologetically.

She laughed. 'No, really, you do look a bit like a gipsy. It must be the beard and those dark smouldering eyes.'

'Don't forget the hooked nose,' I said, following her mood.

'Oh yes, that too.'

It's all true actually; my grandfather was a Cornishman and I take after him. But only in appearance. People soon realize that I'm nothing like as tough as I look.

'Seriously, though,' she continued, 'don't you find it a bit cold sometimes, at this time of year?'

I had begun to explain my plans for dealing with this, when some of the other staff arrived and there was the usual round of introductions.

I didn't dislike Ron at first. He was a fleshy man with a slight over-abundance of North Country charm, but he seemed civil enough. I discovered his less pleasant side later.

After a brief tour of the laboratory he'd set me to work on the urine bench, which was no more than I'd expected. The new boy always gets the piddles.

It was an old, dark, high-ceilinged laboratory, long overdue for replacement; in fact, the floor above, which had been nurses' quarters, was closed off, because it was structurally unsafe. It was quite a comprehensive laboratory, including a virology as well as a bacteriology section, and even a small research unit.

There were about forty staff altogether, but only two faces stuck in my mind that first day. There was the medical director, Dr Peter

Carey, a handsome, distinguished-looking man in early middle age, with the sort of professional charm that I'm convinced is part of the medical school curriculum. And there was John Devlin.

He was shorter than me, shorter than Sally for that matter (I'm five feet ten) with a thatch of sandy hair and blue eyes. The thin chiselled face went with his thick Glaswegian accent.

Ron passed me over to Philip Snow, who passed me over to Sally, which I didn't mind a bit. After getting me started, she would come over periodically to see how I was getting on.

It was just after twelve and she'd taken off her lab coat to go out when I'd asked her about something. She was bending over my bench to show me and so didn't notice John Devlin coming up behind her. Without warning, he smacked her be-jeaned bottom.

She straightened up with a squeal.

'I've told you not to do that!' she blazed. 'You ill-mannered haggis.'

'Right, hen, an' I've told you that I've got just the one hour, an' you're wastin' time.' His accent was more pronounced than ever.

'One day you'll push me too far,' she said, and yet you knew as she said it that that day

32

was a long way off.

'You comin'?'

'Oh, at once, sir. Although perhaps you'll allow me to introduce the person you so rudely–'

'We already met,' he said, not giving me a glance. 'Come on.' He turned away, and with a helpless shrug, she followed.

I had sat there trembling, not knowing when I had ever felt so much like hitting someone, but as I calmed down, I thought...

Yes, he was rude, intolerably rude, and yet...

And she was the first woman I'd warmed to since...

The truth was that I'd felt a flash of jealousy, sexual jealousy, and it was the first time since ... since Jill.

It was so unexpected, so strange.

CHAPTER 2

It had grown colder, and mid-week had brought the harbinger of winter, the first hard frost. It also brought me my first taste of trouble. I'd settled in fairly well, I thought, finding my place among the rhythms and currents that flow through every hospital laboratory. Philip Snow, who was my immediate boss, seemed to be an easy-going enough character on the surface, although underneath you could detect a tension holding his slim frame together, a sort of repressed asceticism. I wondered whether he was part Scandinavian or German; he had very fair hair and pale blue eyes that sometimes burned with a suppressed anger if he heard something he didn't like, deepening the lines in his otherwise attractive face. Still, he didn't bother me.

I've never minded doing urines; it's not exactly your-life-in-their-hands stuff, but you can save a great many patient hours of misery if you do it properly and that gives me satisfaction. The basic principle's the same everywhere: you examine the sample microscopically for pus cells, then culture it on to an agar-plate for bacteria. These don't grow until the following day, and if there are any, you then have to put up further tests to see which antibiotics they're sensitive to. This takes two days, but there are recognized short cuts which can save the patient a day's discomfort.

When you're using a good microscope, it is as though you're down there, inside the material you're examining, and this is how I felt the next day as I examined an obviously infected specimen. It was as though I could reach out and touch the living pus cells and the bacteria that swarmed around them.

I looked at the form. *Female: twenty-four years old, pregnant, back pain, frequency. On ampicillin, query sensitivity.* Just the sort of patient who could use that extra day.

I looked round. The only other person in the lab at that moment was Ian Lambourne, a monkey-faced youth who had married early and was still studying for his Fellowship. I called him over.

'Don't you do Direct Sensitivities here?' I asked.

He shook his head. 'Ron says they're unreliable.'

'Surely that depends on how you do them. Look at that.'

He looked down the microscope and then at the form. 'I see what you mean,' he said, 'but you're preaching to the converted. It's Ron you've got to convince.' He thought for a moment. 'Look, why don't you put up a few comparison plates and show them to him in a couple of days' time. He might listen to you.'

I agreed and during the rest of the day put up Direct Sensitivities on the more obviously infected specimens.

The next day, when the bacteria grew on the primary plates, I prepared conventional sensitivity tests, and on the following day, Thursday, compared them. They gave identical results.

I had intended to catch Ron alone and show him, but Ian, for the best of reasons I suppose, chose to bring it up in the rest-room that morning.

'Ron,' he said before I could stop him, 'I've been thinking. I wonder if it's time we considered Direct Sensitivities again?'

Ron said pleasantly enough, 'We've been over that before, Ian, they're simply not reliable enough.'

'Well, Chris has been telling me how well

they worked in his last laboratory—'

'Oh, has he, now?' said Ron grimly.

I winced and Ian blundered on. 'Yes. He's put up some comparison plates and honestly, you can't tell the difference. Why don't you come and have a look at them after coffee?'

Ron looked at me, then back at Ian. 'The answer's No, for the reasons I've told you before, and the question is closed. Right?'

He turned back to me. 'Who gave you permission to use plates for that purpose?'

'No one did, but—'

'Then I'll thank you not to waste laboratory materials in future, and not to deviate from our laid-down procedures. That clear?'

'Of course, but—'

'You're not a Senior any more. You're a locum and you'd better get used to the idea PDQ.' He turned back to his paper.

I sat in silence. It's not my way to make trouble, to lock horns with my superiors, that's why I became a Senior – but Ron had this supreme gift of being able to ascend the mildest of noses.

'Excuse me, Ron,' I heard myself say. He looked up. 'I obviously owe you an apology for using the plates without asking, but I'd like to point out that I wasn't deviating from your procedures, because I didn't report my results.'

His eyes widened in astonishment. 'Don't argue with me, Chris.'

'I'm not arguing with you, I just–'

'Yes, you are, you're arguing with me. Cut it out, right?'

I shrugged and was about to agree, when John Devlin intervened.

'I don't think he was arguing with you, Ron, he was just trying to make his point.' It was said perfectly politely, and yet it was unmistakably a challenge.

'I don't remember asking your opinion, Mr Devlin.'

'I'm sorry, Ron, I don't want to interfere, it's just that he wasna' arguin', he was just makin' a point. A guid point, as it happens.' The accent grew stronger as he went on.

Ron held himself back with an effort. 'As we already know, Mr Devlin, you were employed directly by Dr Carey for "research" purposes and are responsible to him, so I can't discipline you. But I can insist that you keep out of my affairs. All right?' He stood up as he finished and swept out.

John gave me a wink before turning back to his book.

Friday used to be the day when the younger and more extrovert staff would go to the pub at lunch-time to limber up for the weekend; however, the practice has been discouraged in recent years because of the increased complexity of the work, and latterly the chronic shortage of staff.

John Devlin was evidently an old-fashioned type; he swaggered in at just after twelve to inquire loudly, 'Who's comin' down the boozer, then?'

Sally shot him an irritated glance and Phil quickly crossed over to him.

'For God's sake, John, give them a chance to finish their work.'

John looked round. 'Looks to me as though they have finished.'

He was right and one or two of the juniors were trying to hide grins at Phil's discomfiture.

'Even so,' said Phil, swallowing, 'I'd rather you didn't just come barging in like that … disrupting everything.'

He was quite within his rights, yet still managed to look foolish.

John said, 'Why don't you come with us then, keep the troops in order?'

Phil quickly glanced at Sally, then said loudly, 'I might, at that.'

'You do that,' John said, then turned to me. 'You comin', Chris?'

'I don't think so, thanks.'

He came over. 'Come on, we need you for an antidote.'

'No, thanks.'

He stood over me uncertainly, not used to being refused. Sally, who had been looking distinctly unhappy, said, 'Come on, Chris, it'll do you good.'

'Oh, OK,' I said after a pause, to make it clear that it was she who'd persuaded me.

A few minutes later, I found her waiting for me as I came out of the locker-room.

'Just making sure you don't change your mind,' she said, grinning.

I grinned back, then said, 'I can't understand why John asked me.'

'Oh, that's obvious. He can't bear Ron, so you're automatically his buddy, since you stood up to him yesterday.'

'I'm not sure I want to be his buddy,' I said, buttoning my overcoat. 'Sorry,' I added quickly.

She smiled wanly. 'That's all right.'

'I'm rather surprised that Phil agreed to come,' I continued. 'I wouldn't have thought that was in character.'

'It isn't,' she said curtly, as we made for the

stairs. 'John asked him so as to get at me.'

'Why should that get at you?'

'Oh, never mind.' Her lips tightened, then relaxed into a grin as a tall, dark-haired man emerged from the virology corridor.

'Charles,' she said, 'have you met Chris yet?'

He smiled at me. 'I believe we were introduced briefly by the Herr Gruppenführer, weren't we?' He was very well-spoken, almost self-consciously so. He held out a hand. 'Charles Hampton.'

'Chris Randall.'

'We're going to the Turf for lunch,' said Sally. 'Why don't you come with us?'

'Aren't you going with John?'

'Yes, among others.'

He considered for a moment. 'Well, since you asked me so nicely, why not?'

The others were waiting for us outside.

'About time–' John began, then stopped and scowled as he saw Charles.

We set off. It was one of those beautiful November days that make you forget about frost and winter. The bare knobbly branches of the pollarded limes in the streets stood out against the vivid blue sky, and you could feel the sun on your face and shoulders.

John walked ahead with Ian and two

41

others, a pretty girl called Mary and a boy whose name I forget. Phil was talking to Sally a little way ahead of Charles and me, and as I watched his face, I saw in a flash what Sally had meant. He was crazy about her. It was so obvious that I wondered why I hadn't spotted it before.

Charles was asking me about locum work. I told him briefly, then asked what he did.

'I work for Parc-Reed, the pharmaceutical firm. I expect you've heard of us.'

'Who hasn't? You're a rep, I take it?'

'I am not,' he said frostily. 'I'm a graduate scientist.'

'Oh,' I said, a little taken aback. 'No offence intended. When you meet people from the commercial sector, it's usually safe to assume that they're reps.'

'Maybe so, but I'm not.'

'So what brings a graduate scientist to Oxford National Microbiology Laboratory?'

'I'm installing a comprehensive system of Hepatitis and AIDS testing. We've developed a completely new range of products and Oxford has agreed to run a trial. I usually work in the research labs in London.'

'Oh,' I said again. 'Sounds interesting.'

'It is.' We walked a few more paces, then he said, 'Did you go to University? I know some of you people have degrees these days.'

'No, I didn't, although our Institute Fellowship is generally accepted as a degree equivalent now.'

'I wouldn't necessarily agree with you there.' He smiled tolerantly. 'I don't blame you, or your Institute, for trying it on, but we both know that your Fellowship can't compare with a good degree.'

'I dare say you're right,' I said easily. 'It rather depends on what you call a good degree, though. How many universities in this country produce decent Science graduates these days? Half a dozen?'

He chuckled. 'Oh, I'm sure you've got a point there.'

'Where did you get your degree?' I asked innocently.

He looked around. 'Here in Oxford. That college over there, actually, Sarum.' He pointed to an ancient ivy-clad gateway, through which you could see a grassed quadrangle. 'Would you count that among your decent ones?'

Well, I suppose I'd walked into it.

John fell back and joined Sally. Her face brightened as Phil's grew darker. It was imperceptible – unless you knew.

'I wasn't trying to be offensive,' Charles

was saying to me.

'Sorry?'

'No offence intended.'

'Oh. None taken.'

We walked in silence for a short while, then he said, 'How long will you be working here?'

'Until Christmas, or so Ron indicated.'

'Seems a long time to be away from home, though I suppose you go back at weekends. Are you married?'

'Not any more.'

He gave a short laugh. 'Join the Club! Where is home?' I told him and his face broke into a smile. 'Small world, I went to school near there.'

He'd been to one of the public schools scattered around Somerset. We exchanged a few remarks about the area, then he suggested we go for a drink one evening the following week. I didn't particularly want to, but it seemed churlish to refuse, so I accepted.

We were crossing a wide tree-lined street with old-fashioned shop windows along the far side, when I noticed a white cross embedded in the tarmac.

'I wonder what that is,' I said idly.

'That's a piece of Oxford history. You

remember Bloody Mary who burned the Protestants?'

'Vaguely.'

'Well, that's where the Bishops Ridley and Latimer were burned at the stake for refusing to accept the Catholic faith.'

Sally and John had fallen back so that they were just ahead of us and I heard John mutter something that sounded like 'Serve the stupid fools right.'

'I beg your pardon?' inquired Charles coldly. 'Oh, of course, you're Catholic, aren't you?' He made it sound like an illness.

John turned and their eyes met briefly and expressionlessly.

'I don't have a religion,' he said. 'What I meant was, how stupid to die for so meaningless a principle.'

Charles ignored this and we walked on.

We turned into an alley named St Helen's Passage. Some wag had inserted the word 'back'. It widened into a courtyard of which the Turf Tavern formed one side. It was old and crowded. We ordered food and beer and found a table.

'I needed that,' said John as he finished some minutes later. He stood up and bought another pint, then sat down and lit a cigarette.

'Not while the rest of us are still eating,' said Sally.

'Why not? It's a free country, isn't it?' He blew an elegant smoke ring.

'Surely freedom relies on self-restraint by the individual,' said Charles conversationally. 'In other words, good manners.'

'My God, he's got a conscience,' said John, looking around. 'We'll be makin' a socialist of him yet.'

Charles's eyes hardened but Sally intervened before he could say anything.

'Oh, shut up and stop acting like schoolchildren, both of you.' She turned to me. 'Talking of history, which you and Charles were earlier, did you realize you were sitting on a piece of history?'

'Really?' I peered down at my chair.

'No, you fool,' she said, laughing. 'This pub, the Turf Tavern.'

'Oh. No, I didn't know.' I smiled back at her.

'Well, you obviously haven't read your Thomas Hardy. This is where Jude the Obscure got drunk after being turned down by Bibliol College; he stood on that table and recited the entire Creed in Latin to the students, 'cos they didn't believe he could do it.'

'What, that very table?'

'Well...'

'It was the most profound part of the book,' said John, who obviously couldn't bear to be left out of anything. 'Jude was more intelligent than any of the students there, but they turned him down because he was working-class. At least that doesn't happen so much now.'

'Yes,' said Charles, 'Hardy made that point very well, but I can't help feeling that the pendulum has swung too far the other way now.'

'How do you mean?' said John without looking at him.

'I mean the so-called positive discrimination policy some universities have these days. The selection of obviously inferior minds because they happen to come from an ethnic minority, or a disadvantaged background.'

This remark was so obviously pointed that when John's reply came, it was almost an anti-climax. Still not looking at Charles he said, 'So the world should be deprived of a potentially brilliant scientist whose only fault is that his parents couldnae afford to have him trained to pass exams.'

'That's emotive as well as irrelevant,' said

Charles. 'The best scientists will always come out on top whatever their backgrounds.'

Now John turned and faced him with a savage grin. 'You're dead right there, Charlie-boy, dead right.'

Charles's face went very still.

Phil said suddenly, 'I agree with John,' and we all looked at him. 'I mean,' he continued, 'we should all have the chance to prove ourselves, shouldn't we? I know I'm glad of the chance Dr Carey's given me to study for my Master's degree–'

'I wasnae referring to you, laddie,' said John, shaking his head. 'We canna have you lab boys tryin' to make silk purses outa sows' ears, can we, Charles?'

Phil said hotly, 'Whatever you think of us, we provide a vital service, don't we, Sally?'

'I think,' she said slowly, 'that the medics on the wards have become so accustomed to having a good laboratory service that they couldn't do without us now.'

'That's just it!' cried John. 'They're *accustomed* to you. They havena realized yet that they don't need you. One day–'

'Rubbish!' said Phil.

'Oh? Now be serious, Phil, just for a moment. When did you last truly save someone's life?'

'Last week,' he replied defiantly.

'I saved one, not long ago,' I said, looking at John.

After a pause he said, 'An' you want to tell us about it?'

'Not particularly.'

'Oh, tell him,' said Sally, 'if it's a chance to put him in his place.'

I moistened my lips, wishing I hadn't spoken.

'It was my neighbour in Watchport, his son, rather. He's an Italian barber, my neighbour, that is. Got three sons.' I took a mouthful of beer to gather my thoughts.

'Anyway, he came to me one night, when I was on call, asking if he should call a doctor for the youngest – hadn't got used to the NHS, even after five years in this country. Anyway, I told him I wasn't qualified to give an opinion, and if he was worried, to just get one. But he begged me to look at the boy, so I did.

'He was barely conscious, delirious and muttering about a terrible pain in his head. As you know, there's been a lot of meningitis about, and if he had it, there wasn't much time, so we drove him straight to my hospital. I told the Houseman I'd wait in the lab.

'Sure enough, some twenty minutes later, some spinal fluid arrived and I ran the fastest batch of tests I've done in my–'

'Surely,' interrupted Phil, 'they had given him Chloramphenicol?'

'They had.'

'Then you needn't have panicked. Chloramphenicol would have taken care of the bacteria, whatever they were.'

'Listeria?' I said, reflecting that Phil was now undermining his own case because he couldn't resist showing off his knowledge.

He gaped at me. 'He had Listeria meningitis?'

'I was trying to tell you. I thought they were funny-looking pneumococci when I first looked down the microscope, it wasn't until I made a wet prep and saw the way they moved that I realized.'

'If they'd left him on Chloramphenicol,' said Phil, 'he'd have died.'

'Exactly. As it was, they changed to penicillin and he lived – just.'

I looked at John. 'I'd say it was the laboratory that saved him, wouldn't you?'

I was half expecting a round of sarcastic applause but all he did was to nod slowly.

'I take your point,' he said. He looked up. 'One of my brothers died of meningitis.'

'I'm sorry,' I said. As I spoke, I realized that his accent hadn't been anything like so prominent.

'Well, it does go to prove what I was saying,' said Phil. 'Anyway,' he added quickly, standing up, 'it's time we were getting back.'

'It only proves that the exception proves the rule,' said John, accent firmly back in place.

As we walked back to the hospital, I thought about Joe and his tragi-comical gratitude, and looked forward to seeing him that evening.

'I cutta your hair my fren', for nothing, for ever!'

I grinned to myself – perhaps I'd buy him a drink that night, except that he'd insist on paying.

The trouble was, I didn't like the way he cut my hair, but was morally obliged to let him–

'That anecdote you told just now – interestin'.'

'Eh?' Jolted out of my reverie, I looked up to see John. 'Oh, thanks.'

'I mean it.' He kept step with me in silence for a moment. 'I don't mean to denigrate all medical laboratory staff,' he said, 'it's just that I can't take bullshit. Makes me react.'

I looked at him, wondering why he was telling me this.

He said, 'Fancy a beer tonight?'

'Afraid I can't,' I said, wondering why I was suddenly so popular. 'Going home tonight.'

'How about next week, then?'

'Oh, all right,' I'd said, unable to think of an excuse quickly enough and lacking the moral courage just to say no. Perhaps he'd forget.

But he hadn't forgotten and that's how it had begun.

CHAPTER 3

Sleeping in Bile may have more pro's in the summer, I thought at about five o'clock, but a definite con is that you can be woken by the morning chorus. Eventually the birds calmed down a bit and I drifted off again until about eight.

It was a beautiful May morning. I washed, had breakfast, and drove to work. I looked into John's lab first but he wasn't there and neither Ron or Phil had heard from him.

When I asked Sally whether she had any idea of his whereabouts, she said, 'Well, he never bothered to tell me anything before, so he'd hardly tell me now, would he?'

'I hope he's all right.'

'Of course he's all right, it's not as if this is the first time he's disappeared for a day or so, is it? Bet you anything he's in tomorrow.'

'Hmm.' I looked up. 'Are you still free tonight?'

She grinned and nodded.

'Good,' I said.

I worked until just after ten, then went for

coffee. After I'd poured it, I looked around.

'Has John Devlin said anything to any of you about where he might be?' I asked.

Ron said his piece about Mr Devlin's manners again, otherwise heads were shaken, no's murmured and eyes lowered.

Except for one pair. Dave, the data-processing man. He stared at me thoughtfully, not bothering to look away when I noticed, so that I was forced to lower my eyes first.

It made me feel uncomfortable for some minutes after.

About half an hour later I was crossing the corridor when my name was called.

'Can you spare me a moment?' It was Dr Carey.

'Certainly.'

He ushered me into his office, closed the door and indicated a chair before sitting down himself.

'Well, Chris, it's good to have you back with us again.'

'Thank you,' I said, rather surprised. Medical Directors don't usually notice locum workers.

'What have you been doing with yourself since we saw you last?' His square, handsome face seemed to show a genuine interest, but as I briefly told him, his dark eyes began to glaze over.

'Well, you've certainly kept yourself busy.' He paused. 'I – er – believe you knew John quite well, John Devlin?'

'Yes,' I said carefully.

'You're as close to him as anyone here?'

'We've kept in touch, but perhaps Sally knows him–'

'Yes, I know about Sally. Tell me, did he confide in you at all?'

'In what way?'

'I'd better explain.' He placed his fingertips together in thought for a moment. 'The truth is, I'm in a rather embarrassing position.' He looked up as he spoke, and something in his eyes gave his face, which was normally open, an evasive, almost closed look. 'You know that John was doing some work for me on the AIDS virus?' I nodded. 'Well, I'm supposed to be giving a progress report on it tomorrow at the Central Laboratory in London. John promised me last week to let me have his results yesterday, but as you know, he's not here.' He found my eyes. 'You haven't heard anything from him, have you?'

'I had a letter from him last week, but it implied he would be here.'

'Did it say anything about his work?'

'Er – no,' I lied.

'I see,' he said slowly, as though he were trying to read my mind. 'But you did know that we were working on this project and were going to write it up together?'

'I believe he mentioned it the last time I was here.'

'Ah. Well, you see, I have to produce something tomorrow, but I can't find anything. You wouldn't by any chance happen to know where he might – er – keep records of his work?'

'So far as I know, he kept them here. Have you tried his office?'

'Yes, yes.' Impatiently. 'Er – you don't think he'd have kept them at home, do you?'

'I honestly don't know.' I didn't, either. 'He's never said anything to me about keeping them at home.' Also true.

What John had actually said to me was that he had hidden them *where no one would ever find them.*

'I see,' said Carey, still gazing at me intently. 'Well, if you do get any ideas, I'd be grateful if you'd let me know.'

'Certainly.' I left his room, still puzzled.

Sally wasn't around at lunch-time, so I went to the canteen by myself. I was about half way through when a shadow made me look up. It was Philip Snow.

'Mind if I join you?' He sat down opposite me.

'Don't see you in here very often,' I said.

'No.' He asked me to pass him the salt and after using it, he said, 'Glad to be back?'

'Yes and no.' He raised his eyebrows at that, so I continued, 'Well, I didn't think much of Ron's reaction yesterday, and I'm rather puzzled about John.'

'Well, you know Ron.'

'That's just it, I don't. But then again–' I smiled– 'I suppose I don't really know any of you when it comes to it.'

'That's not really surprising, considering the short time you've spent here.'

'Perhaps not.'

I finished my meal quickly, not wanting to prolong the conversation. As I made to go, he said abruptly, 'I hear you're taking Sally out tonight?'

'We're going for a drink together, yes.'

'She's already been hurt enough by John, I don't want to see her hurt any more.'

'Neither do any of us, Phil.'

'You know what I mean.' He was staring at me with his slightly fanatical expression.

'Listen, Phil, Sally and I are friends, platonic. I'm not looking for that kind of relationship, and I don't suppose she is either. Does that put your mind at rest?'

He didn't answer, just stared disconcertingly, so I got up and left.

The two encounters had shaken me more than I realized, so I went into the pub opposite the hospital for a beer, then took a walk through the back streets beneath the ancient limes, watching the patterns made by the sun in the sappy green leaves and feeling the cobbles pressing through the thin soles of my sandals.

Of the two, Carey bothered me the most – Phil was just jealous.

Carey's questions had scored close to the truth – how much did he really know? I found myself thinking back to the night John had told me what he was really doing in Oxford and how much it meant to him.

I don't know why we'd become friends in spite of all his negative traits – no, that's not true.

But how can I explain?

That second week back in November, I had been out with both him and Charles, and to my surprise, I'd found that I preferred John's company. He was completely different when he was alone.

I suppose what it boils down to is that he

was the first person who'd guessed what I was suffering. He'd been talking in an acerbic but perceptive way about some of our colleagues and was illustrating a point by telling me how Ron had given Ian Lambourne a difficult time when he'd had to get married.

He'd suddenly looked across the table and said, 'You know what I mean. You've been through the hoop too, haven't you?'

'Yes,' I'd replied, and before I knew it, I'd told him everything. It had been an immense relief, like purging a carbuncle.

'How did you know?' I'd asked him later.

'It was in your eyes, man,' he'd said rather mysteriously. Then: 'A guy like you doesn't chuck up a senior post and go on the road without a reason. It was just logical.'

But I always wondered whether it had been some sixth sense, a sympathy between fellow sufferers.

His own story had come out bit by bit. He'd been one of a family of ten, born into the Glasgow sub-culture of Govan, and yet had known from the moment he could think that he was going somewhere.

'Everyone loves the story of the boy who makes it,' he'd said in his cups one night, 'but in reality–' he shook his head – 'it isnae worth it.'

He had been bitterly resented by his schoolmates, friends, brothers, even his father. They'd all tried to hold him back, but he had made it, only to find that he was not really accepted by the group he wanted to be part of.

He'd become engaged to a girl, but she'd broken it off, he claimed after she'd met his family. Imagined or not, it did explain his attitude towards women.

In fact, although I couldn't sympathize with the way he behaved, I could understand.

One night, the three of us (John and Sally often pressed me to go with them, I think their relationship was at a stage where it needed a third person to hold it together) were in the Turl bar in the centre of town. John had drunk more than Sally and I put together and was in a mean mood.

Sally was giving me another History lesson, this time on the subject of St Frideswide.

'She was a Saxon maiden. This area was part of Wessex, you know, and was always being attacked by Mercia. One day a particularly rampant Mercian caught Frideswide, but after he'd had his wicked way with her, a bolt of lightning struck him blind.'

'I thought it was *self*-abuse that made you go blind,' interrupted John.

She ignored him. 'Instead of leaving him to the mercy of the local wolves, she took him to a holy spring and bathed his eyes–'

'And lo! he was cured–' John again– 'An' they married and lived happily ever after.'

'Yes, you killjoy! And yes! People still visit the spring for its magical properties.' She turned to me. 'It's at Binsey, not far from here.'

'You must take me to see it, I love old legends–'

John snorted. 'St Frideswide! St Legswide, more like. I'll bet she knew exactly what she was doing, and I'll bet she never let him forget her saintliness–'

'As a matter of fact they had a very good marriage,' Sally said, winking at me.

'Marriage! It's all you women think about. I'll give it no more than another two generations,' he said pompously, 'before the institution of marriage dies out altogether.'

'Why?' demanded Sally softly.

'S' obvious.' He took a mouthful of beer. 'Women get what they want now, more than ever before – right?'

'Still not enough–'

'The priorities of men and women are so

61

different that if they're both determined to get what they want, they simply can't live together. QED.'

'Rubbish,' I said. 'All it needs–'

'I tell you, women're all the same. Sally's no different. They're attracted by a man's virility, right? Good breeding stock. An' when they've got him, had their babes, what do they do? They castrate him, cut off what they wanted in the first place. An' then a bit later, they mock the poor devil for bein' a eunuch.'

I turned to Sally. 'You don't have to take that, you're worth three of him.'

'More like five.'

John leaned forward. 'She takes it,' he said clearly, '"cos I'm good in bed. And you like it, don't you, Sally?'

Her cheeks reddened, she lowered her face and I could see slits of tears in her closed eyes. Abruptly, she snatched her coat and handbag and was gone.

'You stupid bastard!' I said to him. He shrugged.

I went after her down the narrow street, caught her by some railings in the glow of an old-fashioned street lamp. Touched her shoulder.

'It's all right, Chris,' she said, her breath

condensing in the freezing air, 'it's my fault, it's me, I'm just so stupid to let it get to me.'

'Come on, I'll see you home.'

Without warning, her arms went around my neck and she burst into tears.

She didn't try to say anything, just cried as I stroked her hair, felt her tears and her warm breath ... and the heat rising in my loins.

She stopped as quickly as she'd started and dried her eyes.

'That's better. I'm better now, thanks, Chris. Please don't see me home, go back to John and–'

'Not bloody likely!'

'He needs you more than I do – company, I mean – he's so lonely, that's why he's like he is. Call him a few names if you like, but go back.'

She put her hands on my shoulders and kissed me, her mouth warm in the cold air, then she walked away. I went slowly back to the bar, deep in thought.

There was another drink in front of my seat. He'd known I'd come back.

'You stupid bastard,' I began, never one for originality. 'You–'

'All right, I know. There's nothing I haven't called myself already.'

'But why, John? She didn't deserve that–'

'Leave it!' he snapped. 'I suppose you think she'd be better off with Phil, or you perhaps–' He broke off and stared at me and I felt myself redden.

'Can't think about getting involved with a woman,' I mumbled. 'Not yet.'

'Let's leave it,' he said more gently. 'I know I'm going to lose her soon, but I can't help it.' We drank in silence for a moment, then he said, 'I could love her, you know, but I daren't let her get too close.'

'Why not?'

'My work.' He drained his glass, set it down. 'I want to tell you something,' he said carefully, 'about my work.'

I found myself listening despite everything, his work was something he never talked about.

'Well?' I said at last.

'Don't crowd me.' He lit a cigarette. 'Get me another pint.'

I did, and he said, 'I think – no, I'm sure, I've found a cure for AIDS.'

Well, I'd been expecting something good...

'I found it by accident when I was working at Parc-Reed.'

'You were at Parc-Reed?'

'For a short while.'

64

'Is that why you and Charles don't get on?'

'That mealy-mouthed prat. Calls himself a scientist! What do you know about AIDS?' he demanded abruptly.

'Not all that much, I'm not a virologist. I know it's caused by HIV, the Human Immunodeficiency Virus, which attacks lymphocytes–'

'An' it's gonna hit this country *hard*,' he interrupted. 'Not just poofters and junkies but anybody. You can forget about prevention, there's too many like me who can't keep their wee Robbies to themselves. An' you can forget about a vaccine, too–'

'What's a wee Robbie?'

'Wha'd'ya think?' Impatiently. 'Robbie Burns, he wasnae just our national poet. Forget it, let's get back to vaccines.'

'The virus changes its coat, doesn't it? Like the 'flu virus?'

'Right! Anyway, a vaccine's no good to anyone who's already got the virus. But somethin' that attacks the virus itself ... that's different.'

'And you've found that something?'

'Look, the virus is like this.' He pushed aside his beer mug and started drawing on the table-top with spilt beer. 'You gotta phospholipid membrane like this, it's covered in spikes.' He started drawing them. 'Oh, this is no bloody good!' He rubbed it out and stood up. 'Come on.'

'I could follow that, John–'

'I said come on, I'm gonna show you somethin'.' He pulled on his coat and made for the door.

I followed him out into the frosted night.

He walked quickly and after a few minutes we passed through the hospital gates. When we reached the lab, he thrust his fingers into the letter-box and pulled out the key, which was on the end of a piece of string. A moment later we were climbing the stairs. I followed him through his office to the Electron Microscope room, where he switched on the light and flung his coat on to a chair.

He turned to me. 'Ever used one of these?'

'I've seen one used,' I said, gazing up at the barrel of the microscope, a stainless steel tube four feet high and perhaps six inches wide, rising from a desk-console of grey metal covered in switches and dials. Massive cables fed into the barrel at intervals.

John sat at the console.

'Doesn't it have to warm up?' I asked.

'Not when it's been left on,' he said, grinning.

He pulled a switch and a circle of green

light grew on the screen directly beneath the barrel. It was encased in metal and with glass portholes through which you could see, and the whole structure made me think of the inside of a submarine.

He turned a dial and the light grew in intensity. 'Saturation,' he murmured, half to himself as his hands strayed over the controls on the console. 'Focus. Condenser.' A blurred image of the microscope's filament appeared and disappeared on the screen. 'That's fine.'

He stood up, went over to a drawer and took out a small container. With a pair of forceps he extracted from it a minute circular grid perhaps a millimetre in diameter, which he then teased carefully into a slot in the end of the metal holder about the size of a toothbrush. This he took over to the microscope and inserted into a hole about a third of the way up the barrel. There was a hiss, then the whine of an electric motor.

'Vacuum pump,' he said. 'You always lose some of the vacuum when you put in a specimen.' He sat at the console again and reached for a row of buttons. 'Low magnification first,' he said, pressing one, and the criss-crossed image of the grid leapt on to the screen. 'Kill the light, will you?'

I did so, and the image on the screen became clearer in the darkness. 'Magnification,' he muttered, turning a dial on his right, and with each click the image jumped in size. After two clicks, we were looking at a single square. With another control, he moved the field of view around, searching for a suitable area.

'What magnification is that?' I asked. He indicated a digital reader which read 1000, the upper limit of an ordinary light microscope. 'We'll have to go to about 50,000 to see the virus,' he said. 'Ah, this one'll do.' He twisted the magnification dial again, the image on the screen jumping with the clicks, then began a systematic search of the area he had selected.

'What is the material?' I asked.

'T4 lymphocytes, infected with HIV *in vitro*, pelleted, embedded in resin, then sectioned– Ah!' He manœuvred the image of an intact cell into the centre of the screen; I recognized it as a lymphocyte by its shape and the large single nucleus.

'You can see all the structures,' said John. 'Look. Nuclear membrane, mitochondria, endoplasmic reticulum – this is a good microscope. Let's look at the cell membrane...'

More clicks as he turned the dial, the cell expanded until only a fraction of it was visible, yet the detail was still perfect, and I felt we were walking on hallowed ground, trespassing, prying almost voyeuristically into the cell's most intimate secrets ... now all we could see was the double line of the cell wall across the screen–

'See the bi-molecular structure?' said John. 'Phospholipid, like most cell membranes – right? That's what the virus steals for its own coat as it emerges, so let's go along it until – no, that's not so good...' He tracked along the membrane until a crudely circular structure came into view, clearly outside the cell, yet still connected to it by a strand of membrane.

'Beautiful,' he breathed. He turned to me, his face radiant in the green light from the screen. 'May I introduce you to HIV, the Human Immunodeficiency, or AIDS, virus.'

I gazed at it in silence.

It was just a circle of material, about the size of a two-penny piece on the screen, with another circle inside and a rectangle of denser material in the middle. Another click, and it filled the screen. The magnification indicator read 50,000.

'I'll take you through it,' he said quietly.

69

'Here's the coat–' he pointed to the outer circle – 'stolen from the lymphocyte. It's covered in spikes it uses to attach itself to its next host, but you can't see them. Here–' he pointed to the inner circle – 'the protein core, icosahedral in structure. And here–' the dense material – 'the RNA. But it's RNA with a difference.' He turned to me. 'Before it can insert itself into the cell's DNA, it has to make a DNA copy of itself–'

'Reverse Transcriptase!' I said. 'That's the enzyme it uses, isn't it?'

'Very good – for a bacteriologist.' He swallowed. 'It's that enzyme that everyone's assumed is the Achilles' Heel of the virus. It's what the drug AZT attacks.'

I listened, fascinated. Only the occasional slurred word betrayed the fact that he'd had seven pints of beer.

'Now.' He leaned back. 'Where would you attack it?'

'The membrane?'

'S'been tried. BHT – Butylated Hydroxy- toluene–' he got the words out somehow – 'incorporates into the membrane which then dishrupts – 'cept that it doesn't. Where next?'

'What's wrong with the Reverse Trans- criptase?'

'Nothin', 'cept that the world's best brains've bin workin' on it for three years, an' only come up with Suramin, which doesn't work, an' AZT, which half works. So where?'

'I don't know.'

'Listen.' He leaned forward, his eyes bright, his words clearer again. 'What I found at Parc-Reed was another Achilles' Heel – found it by accident. The viral DNA made by the enzyme inserts into the host cell DNA an' codes for the coat, the core an' the enzyme, right?'

'If you say so.'

'But there's *more* DNA, so-called redundant DNA, that codes for more proteins, only no one knows what they're there for yet. Now, they gotta be there for somethin', right? Nature doesn't make proteins for fun, does it?'

I shook my head.

'Listen – when the virus gets into you – into someone – they get a temperature and a rash, then they get better. 'Cept they've still got the virus lyin' dormant in a few lymphocytes goin' merrily around in their bloodstream. So wha' happens next? I'll tell you – the virus jus' sits there, p'raps for years, hangin' like a Sword of Damocles –

classical education, see? Tha's why these poor devils hang around for so long, waitin'. Waitin' to see whether they're gonna get AIDS.

'An' then in most cases, the virus suddenly starts multiplyin' again – an' no one knows exactly why. The lymphocytes die, an' hundreds of new viruses emerge an' kill hundreds more lymphocytes, an' so on till they're all dead, an' your immunity's buggered an' you die of stupid infections that normally wouldn't hurt a fly.

'But *why?*' As he leaned forward, a speck of saliva touched my cheek. 'I'll tell you; it's those extra proteins, they're regulatory proteins an' *they* control that surge of activity that kills everything. Well, I've found somethin' that screws up one of those proteins. I know which one, and I know how my substance works. But I dunno what that protein's there for.'

He told me how by chance, he'd noticed the virus culture die in the presence of the substance, how he'd isolated it and tried it again and again until he knew how it worked, and I realized as I listened that he'd discovered his substance in the same way that Fleming had discovered penicillin, he'd noticed something strange and his mind wouldn't rest until he'd found out *why.*

'It's fantastic, John, but why didn't you go on working on it at Parc-Reed?'

'They sacked me, di'nt they?' Now that he'd shown me, the drink began to take effect again. 'Di'nt know what I'd found, did they?'

'Why, John? Why did they sack you?'

'Got me hand in the wrong pair o' drawers.' He drew himself up. 'Very proppa firm,' he said in what he imagined to be an English upper-crust accent, 'can't have that sort of thing going on, can we?' He collapsed in giggles and I wondered how I was going to get him home.

Then he said, 'God, Chris, I wanna nail this stuff, I want it more than anything. Tha's why I came here, Carey doesn't know what I'm doin'. Thinks I'm workin' on a new test for the virus–'

'Why don't you tell him, he–'

John snorted. 'You don't know what he's like. He'd pinch it for himself, kick me out once he knew how it worked.'

'But how can you stop him? He's bound to find out.'

John started giggling again. ''Cos I've hidden the data where no one'll ever find it.'

'But what when you've finished, what are

you going to do with it?'

'Thash my secret,' he said. He faced me. 'Don' look at me like that, Chris. I've tried to play it straight all my life, at school, at college, then at Parc-Reed, but what do I get for it? A kick in the teeth 'cos I'm not good enough for them… Well, now I'm gonna keep what's mine.' He started rambling again. 'I got plans … plans…'

I got him out of the building somehow, where the cold air revived him a little. He clung to my shoulder while we walked back to Bile, then I drove him home.

As he staggered through the gate, I wondered how he'd feel in the morning. Needless to say, he was the same as usual, except for a healthy flush around his cheeks.

CHAPTER 4

I got back to the lab in a thoughtful mood and sat working in automatic, going over what John had told me those five months before. I still had no idea where he might have hidden his data.

'I don't think there's much point in setting these up.'

'Mmm?'

It was Ian. 'Not much point in growing these lymphocyte cultures if John won't be wanting them.'

'He might be back tomorrow.'

'Shouldn't think so.'

I swivelled round to face him. 'Why not?'

He considered a moment. 'I've got a feeling we won't be seeing John again.'

'What makes you say that?'

'Well, he was getting pretty fed up. Told me last week that he'd had enough. I think he's the sort of bloke who'd just up-sticks and go.'

'Did he say what he was fed up about?'

'I can't remember exactly.'

'Try, it's important.'

He frowned in concentration. 'It was something like … he was fed up with being made use of. He said he'd been tricked … conned, and he wasn't going to put up with it.'

'Did he actually say he was going?'

'Well, not in so many words.'

I thought for a moment. 'And you'd been growing a lot of cultures for him until then?'

'Tons. Asked him whether he'd been putting them in his sarnies last month.'

'What did he say to that?'

'Laughed and told me to get on with it.'

We grinned at each other, then I said, 'Let's have a look at your work-book a moment.'

I flipped back through the weeks and months; John certainly had used 'tons' of cultures, but then I knew why.

On impulse, I got up and went across to his office. It was quiet and still. I sat at his desk and thought for a moment, then pulled open the filing cabinet and shuffled through the contents.

Yes – this might be it 'HIV: Extraction and separation of antigens, and absorption on to a plastic carrier.' In other words, sticking bits of the virus on to the walls of a plastic plate, the work Carey had given him to do.

I went through the file. John was a neat

worker, it was easy to follow and I began to understand how he'd managed to work both the projects at once. Both required growth of the virus and the extraction of proteins, it was no wonder he'd been able to fool Carey.

But the point was: *had he fooled Carey?*

I stood up, walked through the Electron Microscope room and stared through the glass door of the airlock into the containment laboratory. HIV isn't a very infectious virus, but the consequence of catching it can be so terrible that it has been classified as a Category 3 organism, and needs a fairly high level of security.

My eyes ranged over the equipment on the benches. Unless you examined it very closely, you wouldn't have known exactly what it was being used for, a fact that had helped John disguise what he was doing.

I went back through to the office and picked up the file. Surely Carey would have tried the filing cabinet?

Well, let's find out.

His door was open, he was sitting at his desk checking through a pile of reports and signing them so that they could be sent out.

He looked up as I tapped. 'Come in, Chris.'

I held out the file. 'I think this must be what you're looking for, Dr Carey.'

'Well *done!* Where did you find it?'

He took it from me and became too engrossed to notice whether I replied or not, so I didn't. I watched his face. It clouded with disappointment, which he quickly tried to hide.

'Well, this material is certainly useful, but I have a feeling there's another file.' He looked at me. 'On similar work.'

'Not that I know of, I'm afraid. Do you want me to keep looking?'

'Please, if you wouldn't mind.'

'And if I see him before you, shall I tell him you're looking for him?'

'Er – yes. That might be an idea.'

I returned to my bench.

There was no doubt, he'd already known about the contents of that file, probably had his own copy, since he'd given John the work to do in the first place. In other words, he knew what John was really working on.

Perhaps he'd known ever since the Christmas party.

Just after five I drove round to John's flat again, although with no great hope of finding him. As I walked up to the door, it opened and Dave stepped out. We both froze.

He recovered first. 'Looking for John?'

'Yes.'

'He's not there.'

'How do you know?' And then, because this sounded too hostile, 'D'you know him, then?'

'That's right. He's away this week. Asked me to keep an eye on his flat.' The flat London accent was too smooth, I didn't believe him.

'D'you know where he is at the moment?'

He shook his head. 'Just said he'd be away. None of my business where. All right?'

He made to pass me, but I didn't move. 'You've got a key, have you?'

His eyes narrowed. 'That's right.'

'Well, perhaps you wouldn't mind letting me in for a moment. He borrowed a book that I need back.'

'Sorry, mate, not on. Not without his say-so. You'll have to wait until he's back. OK?'

This time I did let him pass. Although he was slightly smaller than me, there was something about him, like a coiled snake, that said 'Don't touch.'

I drove back to my place beneath the trees and thoughtfully cooked a meal.

Something was wrong. John might not have many friends in Oxford, but surely he wouldn't ask a comparative stranger like Dave to 'keep an eye on' his flat? And wouldn't he have mentioned it to me?

Later, I washed and changed and drove round to Sally's house. She lived in Jericho, a chessboard of Victorian terraces that had had the good fortune to become 'sought after' just before the demolition gangs moved in. You had to admit that the houses, with their gaily painted doors and windowboxes of flowers, looked better than any modern block of flats.

She had changed into one of those loose summery dresses that somehow make you more aware of the figure beneath than the tightest jeans ever can.

'Where would you like to go?' I asked.

'Oh, somewhere out of town. By the river, perhaps. Chris?'

'Mmm?'

'There's something I've always been meaning to ask you?'

'Yes?' Suspiciously.

'Can I have a look round Bile?'

I laughed. 'Be my guest.'

Like a lot of women, she wasn't satisfied until she'd probed every corner of my home.

'It's like a ship's galley,' she said at last. 'So tidy. How do you manage it?'

'You have to be tidy in a small space like this.'

'Most of the men I know would keep it like a pigsty.' She looked at me thoughtfully. 'It's the one thing you and John really have in common. Tidiness, I mean.'

Mention of John started me thinking. 'Sally, was John ever friendly with that data-handling bloke, Dave?'

'He most certainly was not, they had a row last week.'

'What about?'

'Oh, Dave wanted to know something about the terminal in John's room, and John told him to mind his own business. Or so I heard.'

'No chance they knew each other from before?'

'Pretty unlikely. Why?'

I told her about my meeting with Dave at John's flat.

'How odd,' she said.

'Sally, I think there's something funny going on.'

She thought for a moment, then said, 'Would it help if we went round to the flat now?'

'Not much use without a key.'

'I've still got one.'

I looked at her and she shrugged. 'He didn't ask for it back and I certainly wasn't going to offer it. Hang on, I'll get it.' She jumped up and hurried back to her house.

'He wouldn't have had three, would he?' I said a few minutes later as we drove across town.

'Three what?'

'Keys. He'd have asked for yours back if he'd wanted Dave to have one.'

I pulled up outside the front door, locked Bile and followed Sally up the stairs.

Inside the flat, the air held a slight mustiness.

'He must have been here Friday,' said Sally, looking round, 'because he was at work. But it doesn't look as though he's been back since.'

The bed was made up and everything seemed to be neatly in its place. His briefcase lay on the desk by the window, beside the 'phone and a framed photo of his mother.

'Funny,' said Sally, picking it up. 'He's always kept this beside his bed. He's devoted to her, you know.'

'Yes, he told me.' I went through to the kitchen and looked around. Everything had been tidied away. I came out and opened the wardrobe, but couldn't tell whether any of this clothes were missing. Neither could Sally.

I looked under the bed. There was nothing except a screwed-up envelope.

'What's that?' asked Sally as she came over.

'Only an old envelope. Not so old, though,' I said, looking at the postmark. 'He must have got this last week.'

'Let's have a look.' I handed it to her. 'London EC1. From North American Pharmaceuticals.' She looked up. 'Who are they?'

'NAP? Just one of the biggest drugs firms in the world. Sally, d'you mind if I look through his briefcase?'

She shrugged and sat down on the bed. 'You've as much right as me.'

As I unzipped it, two more envelopes with the NAP logo fell out. With a glance at her, I extracted one of the letters.

Dear Mr Devlin,

Thank you for your letter dated 1st May. Please don't misunderstand me, we are most interested in your proposal, but we do feel that some practical demonstration is necessary before we can take it any further. I feel sure we can arrange this without compromising you, as you put it. Perhaps if you would care to visit us again, at our expense, we could discuss the problem.

We look forward to hearing from you.

Yours sincerely

I read it out to her, then looked up. 'That's where he is, London–'

I was interrupted by a rattle as the door swung open. A man in a turban stood in the doorway.

'What do you think you are doing?' he demanded in the sing-song, almost Welsh intonation so many Asians have. 'Tell me or I will telephone the police.'

'It's all right, Mr Singh,' said Sally, and his face sagged with relief as he saw her.

'Oh, hello there, miss. Long time no see.'

'This is a friend of John's. He hasn't been to work this week and we were getting worried. When did you last see him?'

He stepped inside. 'Last Friday, I think. Yes, not since Friday morning.'

'You don't know where he is?' I asked, having slipped the letter back into the briefcase.

'No idea,' he said.

'Has anyone else been up here since then?' asked Sally.

'Not so far as I am aware. I like to know all about all such visits,' he added pointedly.

There was a short silence. He obviously

wasn't going to leave before we did, so I said, 'Well, thanks for your help,' as I tucked the case under my arm and made for the door.

'Excuse me,' he said. 'The briefcase – I believe it belongs to Mr Devlin.'

'Yes,' I said, 'it contains notes of mine from the laboratory…'

'It's what we wanted to see John about,' said Sally.

'Nevertheless, I must ask you to leave it here, please.' He held out a hand.

I stood irresolute for a moment, then Sally said, 'Better give it to him,' so I did.

As we drove away, she said, 'Well, at least he didn't ask me for the key. What now?'

'A drink,' I said.

We went to the King's Arms at Sandford Lock and sat outside, watching the reflection of the sunset in the slowly moving water. I asked if she knew how near John had been to finishing his work.

'He should have finished by now,' she replied. 'He told me just before we split up that another month should do it.' She sat up and looked at me. 'I bet you were right just now. He's got the scent of a really good offer, maybe NAP, maybe another firm, and he's rushed off and forgotten everything else, including you.'

'That doesn't explain Dave.'

'Perhaps not,' she said slowly, 'but I still think that's where he is. You were looking forward to seeing him, weren't you?'

'I suppose so.'

She shook her head slightly. 'It's never ceased to amaze me how you two got on. I mean, you're so different. He's arrogant, selfish, pig-headed–'

'That's because of his upbringing, he–'

'That's all very well, but he's not the only person who's suffered. Is he, Chris?' She let the last three words hang.

'Perhaps that's why,' I said tonelessly.

'Why what?'

'Why we get on.' I looked up. 'People who have … been unhappy sense it sometimes in others. It draws them together. How much did he tell you?'

'Not much. Only that your wife was killed in a car accident and that you blamed yourself.'

'With reason.'

'How long ago was it, Chris?'

'Ten months.'

She touched my arm. 'Whatever happened, you mustn't go on blaming yourself. It's not what she'd have wanted, is it?'

'I don't know.'

Her hand closed over mine and I told her then, in a dry, almost dispassionate way, and yet it was as much of a release as when I'd told John.

She held my hand throughout and when I'd finished, I felt so close to her, closer than I'd been to John. It was sexual without being erotic. She'd listened as only a woman can.

'I'll get you another drink,' she said.

'D'you want to go in?'

'No, let's stay out.'

The sun had set, but its afterglow persisted in the sky over the hill and on the water. When she came back, I asked her how her date with Phil had been.

'How did you know it was Phil?' she demanded.

'I guessed.'

'He told you, didn't he?'

'Unintentionally.'

She said, 'Well, if you must know, he's a very nice person and very good company, except for one thing.'

'He's nuts about you.'

She sighed. 'Is there anything about me you don't know?'

'I saw how he felt about you months ago.'

'Did you! Well, I was going to say that I couldn't reciprocate his feelings for me, which comes to the same thing, I suppose. I shouldn't have agreed to go out with him really, it's only leading him on.'

'Why did you?'

'I like him, I always have. He *is* good company, he doesn't hog the conversation like John.'

'He's always seemed a bit neurotic to me.'

'That's because you've seen him with John, and John brings out the worst in him. Just because he can't think so fast doesn't mean he hasn't got anything interesting to say.'

'John seems to bring out the worst in everyone, doesn't he?' I mused.

'Including you and me?'

I smiled and shook my head. 'We're exceptions. I was thinking about Charles and Ron. And Carey.'

'Why Dr Carey?'

I told her how he'd been asking me to look for John's data.

'D'you think he's known all along what John's been doing?' she asked.

'He must have. Since the Christmas party, anyway.'

Her face cleared. 'Of course! I'd forgotten about that. I've always wondered why he didn't sack John then. But surely John would've had to have told him about it.'

'In that case, why is Carey scrabbling about after the data now? Why should he think I know? He hasn't asked you–' I looked up – 'has he?'

'As a matter of fact,' she said slowly, 'he has. Only I didn't realize at the time. Yesterday. I took him some reports to sign and he started chatting. Asked me if I was happy here, whether I intended to stay. That's when I told him I wasn't seeing John any more, it seemed so natural. Then he asked me if I'd been interested in John's work and I said we hadn't discussed it. Which was quite true, I suppose.

'If he hadn't tried to be so clever, I could have told him where John keeps his data–'

'*Really?*'

'Well, it's blindingly obvious. In the computer.'

'D'you know, I think you're right... I'll check it tomorrow.'

'Of course I'm right. Listen.' She leaned forward. 'John knows that Dr Carey knows and is going to try and force him to publish the data in this country, whereas John wants to sell it abroad. That's why John's disappeared and why Dr Carey is after him. QED.' She sat back. 'I'll bet you anything John 'phones you tomorrow at work, or maybe later in the week.' She held out her glass. 'So you can buy me another drink, and let's not talk about John any more.'

We seemed to have reached a dead-end anyway, so I did as she asked, then said, 'What would you like to talk about?'

'You.' Her face was luminous in the light from the river. 'I've been thinking about you driving around the country in your funny dormobile. D'you think you'll always be a gipsy?'

I shrugged elaborately. 'Who knows?'

'You can't go on doing it for ever.'

'Why not?'

'You just can't. Don't you ever want to get married again?'

Upstream, a moorhen let out its eerie call and a moment later skittered across the water. A bullock coughed on the other bank and laughter rang from another table.

'I'm sorry, Chris, I–'

'No, I don't think so.' I looked up. 'I've had my love-affair. One's enough in a life-time.'

'You haven't got over it yet. I bet you don't even look at other women.'

I smiled to myself, then said, 'Oh, I look all right, it's just that I don't touch.'

'Tell me about Jill,' she said.

Some time later I took her home. She opened the door, then quickly leaned over and kissed the side of my mouth before getting out.

I couldn't sleep when I got back to the trees, but lay thinking about her, then about John and Carey, and then about the Christmas party.

I suppose most work-places try to preserve the façade of camaraderie by doing something at Christmas. Perhaps I've become cynical since Jill died, but these 'Works-do's' always seem so artificial to me.

Sally had gone because she thought she ought to, John because the others didn't want him to, and between them, they cajoled me. It was my last day there, a Friday, and I'd have rather gone home.

Carey had sat at the end of the table and Ron had sat next to him, to underline his position, I suppose. Sally and John were next to Ron and I sat opposite them.

John didn't say very much; in fact, he was a model of good behaviour – until we finished the main course.

Ron had made some comment about Oxford, and Carey was telling him, and the rest of us, how fortunate we were to be living and working here.

'There's a sense of timelessness about Oxford, a sense of History,' he said. 'You can feel it working around you all the time, a sort of eternal fermentation. Some of the world's greatest brains have studied here, perhaps some are now.' He smiled. 'You know, it never fails to give me a lift, seeing the students gowned up in the High on Graduation day, wondering whether there's another Einstein among them.'

'Aye,' agreed Ron, whose style it usually was to rant about the chinless wonders of Christ Church. 'I'm hoping, since we're livin' here now, to get my two into one of the colleges.'

'Ye – es,' said Carey tactfully.

Phil, who was sitting next to me, said, 'It's not quite like that if you've always lived here. I have a sort of love-hate relationship with the place, almost as though it were two towns at once.'

'Ah yes, Town and Gown,' said Carey. 'Inevitable, I suppose. You should be careful, Phil, there are those who would construe that as envy.'

'Oh, but I'm proud of Oxford,' said Phil. 'It's just that sometimes I don't know whose town it is. I was born here, I've lived here all my life, and yet sometimes I feel that it belongs to the students more than me.'

'I'm afraid that's inevitable too, Phil,' said Charles, who was between him and Carey. 'I spent the best three years of my life in Oxford, it's part of me, I always feel as though I'm coming home.'

'But it isn't your–'

'Listen, Phil, every town has to have its *raison d'être*, and Oxford's is the University, with the rest of the town as its service area. It works both ways, you wouldn't have a job here if it wasn't for the University; in effect, you owe your livelihood to it.'

'I know all that,' said Phil impatiently. 'It's just that sometimes I feel like a stranger in my own town, as though I didn't belong.'

'You don't,' said John suddenly. 'What d'you expect? It's your own fault.'

'That's an interesting observation,' said Charles smoothly. 'His own fault. How do you work that out?'

'It's a question of attitude, isn't it?' replied John just as smoothly, and Sally shot him a warning look. 'Think about it,' he continued. 'The natives, like Phil here, have had to play host for centuries to the world's best brains, that's what you said, isn't it, Dr Carey? To the Elite. Had to put up with their behaviour. Have you ever seen them spraying the passers-by with champagne on Graduation day? Have you ever–?'

'Just youthful high spirits,' cut in Carey, 'a release after years of study.'

'If it were punks doing it, they'd be arrested for threatening behaviour.'

'It's not the same thing – students aren't intimidating like punks. But pray don't let me interrupt your – er – thesis.'

'Thank you,' said John politely, and anger shadowed Carey's face for a moment. 'Where was I? Oh yes … the natives, like poor Phil here, they've had to put up with *you* lot–' he nodded to Charles – 'for generations.' He turned back to Phil. 'Your town's taken away from you and your women impregnated. They use you as lackeys, and you've had to smile and pretend you like it. For centuries. Then with a "ta very much" they're off to pastures new an' the next lot come in. I'm not surprised you feel like you do.'

There was a chuckle from Ian, who was the other side of me, otherwise silence. Phil's face set like stone.

Charles said, 'Now, that *does* rather sound like envy to me.'

'What do I have to be envious of?'

'Not having been to a decent University.'

94

'But I have – Strathclyde.'

'Most people wouldn't agree with you.'

'Perhaps it's irrelevant – surely the goods are more important than the wrappings they come in?'

'Which is why Parc-Reed felt they could dispense with your services, I expect.'

'Oh, do shut up, you two,' said Carey tiredly. 'It's Christmas, remember?'

John was staring in astonishment at Charles. Then he said, 'There's only one thing wrong with Parc-Reed.'

'And you can't wait to tell us,' said Charles.

'The name's spelt backwards.'

There was another chuckle from Ian as he worked it out.

'Mr Devlin,' said Carey. 'I thought I told you to be quiet. If you can't, I suggest you leave.'

John shrugged and didn't say any more, and gradually, the conversation rose to its former level.

When the last course was finished and brandies had been served, Carey cleared his throat. 'I think I ought to propose a toast.' He thought for a moment. 'I propose a toast to – er.'

'The natives of Oxford,' said John, raising

his glass to Phil.

Phil went white. 'Don't *you* call *me* a native,' he said between his teeth; then, without warning, threw the contents of his wine-glass in John's face.

Fortunately, there wasn't much left. As John reached for his table napkin, Charles said, 'I rather think you asked for that.'

'I'm inclined to agree,' said Carey. 'Apologize to Phil before you go, will you?'

'Sure.' John got to his feet. 'Sorry, Phil, nothin' personal.' He turned to Charles. 'One day, punk, your firm's gonna find out what they missed when they sacked me.'

'Bravado.'

'When you get back, look up the records of my research. Ask yourself, where was it leading? Ask yourself how long–'

'Get out!' Carey almost screamed.

You fool! I thought silently. A moment later, Sally got up and followed him.

I'd left the following day, and so didn't hear what had happened until two months later when John wrote to me. Carey had given him a week's notice, but had then relented, provided John wrote an apology and pinned it on the noticeboard. This, to my amazement, John had done. It was almost as if they needed each other.

96

CHAPTER 5

The next day, Wednesday, I went to John's office as soon as the rest of the staff were having coffee, sat down at his desk in front of the terminal and wondered how to make it work.

Unlike me, John had had an empathy with computers that was almost frightening, and as though they acknowledged this, he could do almost anything with them.

I found the main switch, and when the cursor on the screen glowed, pressed Return.

'Log-on,' the screen told me.

What was John's code? Probably his initials, JSD123 – but surely, he'd have changed that by now...

I tried it.

'Enter program required.'

Oh well, I found the menu and then R for Research.

The screen flickered, then said: 'HIV Protein Structure Projects,' and underneath, 'Password?'

I sat back and thought.

John loved reversing things, so I tried 123JSD.

WRONG! said the screen triumphantly and the program crashed.

I started at the beginning again, and this time tried 321DSJ.

Yes! But instead of the data, a message flashed on and off the screen: 'Program at present locked by another user.'

My scalp tingled. *Someone in this building, now, was looking at John's data.*

How many terminals were there?

Six, I thought: This one, Main Lab, Virology, office; Carey and Ron had one each – Carey! He'd had the same idea...

I got up and went into the corridor. Carey's door was shut – it was him, it had to be! Better check, though.

Virology was empty, and so was the main office.

Ron's door was ajar. I thought of an excuse and knocked. No answer. I looked round the door. Empty.

A glance told me that the main lab was empty too. Except for one person, sitting at the terminal.

Dave. Even from behind, I recognized him instantly. He scribbled something on a pad beside him, then turned back to the keyboard. Tapped, then swore softly as the screen flickered and the program crashed.

But surely, if he already had the password–

Without warning, he swivelled round and our eyes met.

I should have just walked in, said I'd come to fetch something, but I didn't. I panicked, turned, and walked swiftly back to John's office.

You *fool!* I thought.

The door opened and he came inside. He must have run, although I hadn't heard him. The door clicked shut.

I backed away as he moved silently across to the terminal. He glanced at the message still flashing on and off and then looked at me.

'I'm doing some work on John's program for him,' he said softly, as, catlike, he approached. 'It's between me and him.' He was close to me now, but seemed to move ever closer.

'Between me and him,' he repeated, 'and that's how it stays until he's back. Ask him then if–'

'Where is he?'

'I said, ask him then if you want to know, but until then, keep out of his business–'

'Where is he?'

'That means off his computer programs,' he continued in the same soft voice. 'Away from his address, and stop asking questions about him. That clear?'

'Why should–?'

'Is – that – clear?' Still soft, but loaded with such intensity that I just nodded.

'Good. All you have to do is mind your own business and you an' me'll get along fine. All right?'

'Yes.'

'Good.' He turned and walked out of the room, switching off the terminal on his way.

I sat shaking for about five minutes, maybe longer. Staff came back up the corridor from the rest-room, chatting as they returned to their various laboratories. I made an effort to pull myself together, then opened the door and stepped out.

Would he still be in the main lab? Probably not, now that the others were back. I put my head round to check. He wasn't there, but Sally was, so I went over to her.

'I've got to speak to you.'

She looked up in surprise.

'Something really weird's going on and I seem to be in the middle of it...'

'Sorry, Chris, but can it wait till lunch-time? I've this lot to get through.' She indicated a large pile of specimens beside her.

'OK, but–'

'Ah, there you are,' said a voice behind me. Ron. 'I've been looking for you. Would you come along to my office, please?'

I followed him back down the corridor.

'Shut the door, will you?' he said when we were inside. 'Take a seat.' He sat down behind his desk. 'I've been meaning to have a word.'

Having got that far, he didn't seem to know how to go on for a moment.

'I've nothing personal against you,' he said at last, looking up. 'Nothing. But let's be honest, you don't fit in here, do you?'

'I wasn't aware of it,' I said slowly. 'Anyway, it's not as if I'll be here for very long, is it?'

'That's what I wanted to speak to you about. I've got someone else starting here next week, so I won't be needing you any more.'

I shrugged. 'Fine.'

'The point is, you're not very busy at the moment, are you?'

'Busy enough.'

'We don't really need you. Why don't you

do yourself a favour and leave today?'

I gaped at him.

'It's all right, you'll be paid for the whole week.'

After a pause, I said, 'That's very ... generous of you, Ron, but really, I don't mind staying until the end of the week.'

'Well, to be blunt, I don't think you're a good influence here. You unsettle the staff. I'd rather you left now.'

This was so nonsensical that I didn't know what to say for a moment. Then:

'Ron, I just don't understand this. How do I unsettle the staff?'

'Well, for a start, you won't leave Sally alone. Just now, for instance. I can't find you where you're supposed to be, no, because you're interfering with Sally again.'

'But I've only been here a couple of days, so—'

'Exactly. It was bad enough when Mr Devlin was all over her.' He was speaking faster now. 'One of the best workers we've had, until *he* came along. And now she's seen through him at last, you come back and—'

He stopped himself abruptly, then said in a calmer voice, 'I want you out.'

'All right, but why don't you let me stay until the end of the week?'

'Because I want you out now.'

Why argue any more? 'OK Ron,' I began tiredly, but was interrupted by a knock at the door.

'Come in,' Ron called.

It was Ian. 'Oh, there you are,' he said when he saw me, 'I've been looking for you. Ron, we've got a problem.'

'Well?'

'Nearly all the cell cultures we're supposed to be using tomorrow have failed. Contamination, by the look of them.'

Ron's face twisted towards me. 'I knew you'd be more trouble than you're worth—'

'Wait a minute, Ron,' said Ian. 'These cultures were set up on Friday, so it couldn't have been Chris. It was either me or Val. Me, probably,' he added gloomily.

Ron just looked at him.

'The point is,' Ian continued, 'the virology lab are going to have to go easy on what cells we've got, and if Val and Claire are still off tomorrow, I'm going to need some more help.'

You could feel the cogs turning in Ron's brain as he looked from one to the other of us.

'We've got another locum coming next week,' he said at last. 'A virologist this time, so that should help. I'll go and tell Virology not to use too many cells.' He paused, then: 'You and Chris will have to do what you can for now.'

My lips began framing the words: But, Ron, you said just now you wanted me out – however, I thought better of it.

He glanced at me as though he knew what I was thinking. 'Well, you'd better go and get on with it, hadn't you,' he said.

When we got to the cell lab, I told Ian what he'd interrupted.

'But that's crazy,' he said in disbelief. 'Why has he got it in for you so much?'

'I only wish I knew.'

'Oh well, we'd better do as the man said and get on with it.'

We made a good team and worked solidly for the rest of the morning, and by the time Sally came for me at one, we'd caught up with nearly a quarter of the backlog.

'Are you coming?' she said. 'I've got to be back by half past.'

I looked at Ian, who said doubtfully, 'We've still got a hell of a lot to do.'

Sally said, 'Oh, come on, Ian, we'll only be twenty-five minutes.'

He grinned. 'All right. After all, who am I to stand in the way of love's young dream?'

Sally strode in and pretended to hit him.

'Mercy!' he screeched, covering his head with his hands. She stopped and he gave me a broad wink.

'Ah,' he said, 'methinks the lady doth protest too much,' and nimbly leapt from his seat to avoid another assault.

'Well, *are* you coming?' Sally demanded.

'Can't say I envy you,' said Ian from a corner, 'she's even worse than my missus.'

Sally shot him a look of withering contempt and made for the door.

'Well, what was it you wanted to tell me?' she said as we emerged into the sunshine.

I had just started, when as though by magic Phil appeared beside us. 'Going to lunch? Mind if I join you?'

'Of course not,' said Sally.

As we approached the canteen, he said to me, 'Sally's been telling me about your dormobile.'

'Oh?'

'It's all right at this time of year I suppose, but it can't be much fun in the winter.'

'It's OK,' I said tonelessly.

He kept up a flow of chatter throughout the meal while I sat writhing inside with irritation. Then he switched back to my own arrangements.

'Beats me how you manage to find anywhere to park for the night in Oxford,' he said. 'Wouldn't have thought there was much available space left.'

'There's always somewhere if you're prepared to look.'

'Where are you staying at the moment?'

'By the canal. There's a small car park beside Port Meadow.'

'Oh, I know, over a hump-back bridge, isn't it? Surrounded by trees.'

'Yes.'

'Well, rather you than me.' After a pause, he turned to Sally. 'About tonight, did you have anything in mind?'

'Not really.'

'I thought we might hire a punt,' he said, smiling, 'go up to the Viccy for a couple of drinks.'

She smiled back. 'Why not? It sounds nice.'

So much for not leading him on, I thought. Although perhaps she wanted to put me in my place after what Ian had said.

Then I remembered promising Ian I wouldn't be long, so I made my excuses and left.

We spent most of the rest of the afternoon trying to make up for the failed batch of cells. Twice I tried to catch Sally alone, but on both occasions someone appeared beside us, almost as though it were planned.

A slow anger ignited inside me. Something was wrong! It was as though John had never existed, and I was an embarrassment because I was a reminder of him.

I had to look at his computer again.

But how? Dave seemed especially ubiquitous, pausing as he passed our doorway, or watching me over his coffee-cup.

Could I come back tonight? I knew where the key was hidden – no, there was no need. I'd do it after everyone had gone.

But wouldn't Dave realize I was still there, if he saw Bile still sitting in the car park?

I went out after coffee, drove to another car park and slipped back without anyone noticing.

Where should I wait?

Not John's office, Dave might check there. How about the store in the basement? Or better still, the empty floor above.

At five o'clock I slowly finished off what I was doing, so that by the time I changed my coat, nearly everyone had gone.

I sauntered out to the landing. Attached to the tapes across the stairs leading up was a notice: 'Danger – upper floor unsafe.'

I looked quickly round, then ducked underneath and took the stairs two at a time until I was out of sight, then slowly climbed the rest until I reached the next landing, where I stopped beside a window. The sill was thick with dust and the air hot in the afternoon sun. A large fly buzzed at the glass.

I stared out over the city. The building was high enough to give the same view as one of the tourist towers, Carfax or St Mary's. Dreaming Spires rose out of a bed of ancient rooftops. I thought of Sally and the day we'd first met. The fly still buzzed. On impulse, I released the catch and forced the window up enough for it to escape.

Then I turned and wandered across the landing. Half way were doors with more warning notices on them. New hasps had been screwed into the woodwork and fastened with brass padlocks.

I touched one, picked it up. It was heavy, good quality, and had 'Made in England' stamped underneath. Stir of patriotic pride.

Why such a good lock? I wondered, when a hammer and chisel, perhaps even a good pull, would have the hasp out?

I tugged experimentally, and to my astonishment it came free, the four screws just slipping out of the wood. I tried the handle and the door opened.

I glanced at my watch. Twenty past, I needed to wait another ten minutes anyway. Curiosity overcame me and I stepped inside.

A long corridor stretched away, lit by a window at the far end. The air was thick and fusty. There were doors at regular intervals on both sides, some of them open.

I wandered into the first room on the right. It was completely bare except for a washbasin, a couple of fitted cupboards and a boarded-up fireplace.

I tried the next. It was the same, except that my feet scrunched in pieces of plaster on the floor. I looked up to see where they had fallen from the ceiling.

The next room boasted an empty bed-frame, and the one after that, a frame with a mattress. A pair of shoes lay beside a pile of rags in the corner and an enamel mug and an old Thermos flask stood on the window-sill. Builders' detritus.

I walked slowly down the rest of the corridor, glancing into each room, until a groan from the floorboards made me step back hastily. I glanced at my watch. It was nearly half past, time to go back anyway.

I replaced the screws in the hasp, leaving it looking as solid as ever, and went back down the stairs to the laboratory.

It was quite empty. I sat at John's desk, found the switch, and the blank screen of the computer sparked into life. I retraced my steps from the morning and tapped in his code again, backwards. 'Project I,' the screen informed me. 'Do you wish to print?'

I pressed 'Y', the screen flooded with data and the printer whined into life. I kept it going, but as I looked more closely, I realized that it was the same work that was in the file I'd given Carey yesterday, only in more detail.

At last the screen read, 'Project I finished. (C)ontinue for Project II.'

Shaking slightly with excitement, I pressed 'C'.

'Password?' I hesitated, then keyed in the reversed code again.

'WRONG! TRY AGAIN,' flashed the screen, then went blank as the program crashed.

I switched the computer off, on again, then repeated the procedure until again 'Password?' leered mockingly at me.

I sat back and tried to put myself in his place.

John Devlin didn't work, nor John, nor Devlin, Glasgow or Scotland. Nor did they work backwards.

Middle name … something Scottish, S … Stuart!

But neither that nor its combinations worked either.

At last I gave it up, rolled up the paper from the printer and thrust it into my jacket pocket. Then I let myself out into the warm evening air, and deep in thought, strolled over to Bile.

Project II must refer to substance X, the AIDS cure – small wonder he'd hidden it so well. More possibilities for the password filtered through my head: combinations of Sally's name, perhaps…

As I inserted the key into Bile's door, the roll was snatched from my pocket and Dave said, 'You just don't listen, do you?'

CHAPTER 6

As I spun round and saw him, another part of me wondered at the rage swelling in my head. He just stood there looking at me, the printout in his hand.

'Give that back now.' The words forced themselves through my teeth.

'I warned you,' he said flatly, his eyes measuring me.

With a growl, I lunged for it – his hand flashed and his fingers sunk into my belly.

I doubled over, coughing and clutching. His hand went up, but instead of hitting me, he seized my collar and pulled me upright.

'I warned you,' he repeated. 'Now, why don't you be a good boy, take your money and piss off like Ron said.'

'Piss off yourself,' I groaned, pure bravado.

With a tinny bang, he shoved me back against Bile.

'Maggots like you and Devlin, you never learn, do you? Now, keep out of my way in future, right?'

When I didn't answer, his hand tightened. 'Right?'

'All right!' I choked. He let go, and without another word, walked away.

As I leaned back, trying to recover my breath, a white-coated figure hurried over. 'Are you OK?' He touched my shoulder.

I nodded, still unable to speak. He quickly examined my neck, then ran professional fingers over my scalp.

'Well, there doesn't seem to be any damage. Someone you know?'

'Sort of.'

'Well, it looked like assault to me.' He hesitated. 'I know it's none of my business, but if you want to go to the police, you can use me as a witness.' He took a card from his top pocket and scribbled on it. 'My name's Dr Wood. You can always find me at this number.'

I thanked him, climbed painfully into Bile and drove away.

For once, my place in the trees wasn't a haven. The trees were just trees in the evening sky, as unreal as everything else around me. The pain in my stomach slowly subsided, but I couldn't eat.

I drank coffee, sat down. Stood up again and paced Bile's narrow floor. What had

Dave meant, maggots like me and John? Where was John? Should I go to the police as the young doctor had said? And tell them what?

What I really needed was someone to talk to, but there was no one. I couldn't talk to Ron or Carey. Sally was probably trailing her hand in the water by now, from a punt with Phil. Ian?

No, Ian had troubles enough of his own…

I had to walk, just walk and think.

I went across the meadow. Until Jill had died, I'd never really needed anyone to talk to like this because I'd always managed to avoid trouble, or slide around it. Perhaps I should do that now, I thought … take the money and go.

I found myself in the Perch. The beer went straight through my empty stomach to my head.

If I did go to the police, I could use Dr Wood as a witness to Dave's threats.

I bought another pint. If Sally came with me, we could present enough evidence to warrant them looking into it, surely? Perhaps they could trace John.

Another point. Who was Dave to push me around? Owed it to my self-respect to stay. I'd talk it over with Sally tomorrow and at lunch-time we'd go to the police station.

My mind went over and over this until, some time later, I stumbled back through the dusk to Bile, where I fell almost instantly to sleep.

The storm grew louder and rain poured in through the roof – Bile rocked as the torrent bore us downstream. We were sinking…

'Open up! Come on, we know you're in there!' Someone banging on the door. I froze. Dave and his friends?

'Open up, it's the police!'

Bloody hell! I fell out of bed, groped my way over to the door and opened it.

A torch blinded me and a disembodied voice said, 'Took your time, didn't you?'

I put out a hand as though to ward off the beam. 'I was asleep. What do you want?'

'Are you the owner of this vehicle?' I could make out two shadowy forms behind the circle of light.

'Yes. What do you want?'

'Well, you're breaking the law, my lad. We've had complaints about you.'

My head reeled. 'I'm – I'm sorry. Could you turn that torch off, please?'

'How long have you been here?'

The glare was burning my eyes. 'Look,

why don't you come in?' I stepped back and found the light switch.

'Come on, Jim,' said the other one. The torch went out as they clambered up the steps and pulled the door closed behind them.

They were both over six feet, heavy in their dark uniforms, but at least I could see them now.

'Won't you sit down?'

'We prefer to stand, thank you, sir. Now, how long have you been staying here?'

I sat on the bed, feeling naked in my pyjamas. 'This is my third night. Nobody's complained to me, and–'

'That's not the point, sir, you're breaking the law.'

'Which law?'

'Vagrancy Act,' said the other promptly. 'I'm afraid we must ask you to leave. Now.'

'Oh, come on, where am I supposed to go?'

'That's your problem, sir,' said Jim.

'Anywhere outside the County boundaries,' said his friend.

I sighed. 'Look, I'm sorry if I've broken the law. I'll go, of course, but can't you let me stay until tomorrow? I'm not doing any–'

'No, you leave now,' said Jim, making for

the door.

'I'm sorry, sir,' said the other. 'We've been told to make sure you're outside County limits tonight and not parked anywhere illegally.' He followed Jim to the door. 'You'd better get dressed.'

They waited outside while I pulled on some clothes, then followed me as I drove over the bridge.

God, I was tired! My eyelids felt like sandpaper and I'd certainly fail a breathalyser – *perhaps that's what they want!*

Their headlamps blazed in my door mirror. Where the hell can I go? Even if they don't stop me, I won't make it to the next county...

Instinctively, I drove to the only shelter I knew. Sally's home in Jericho. They drew up behind me as I switched off the engine, then Jim was beside me.

'You can't stop here.'

Quickly, before they could think of the breathalyser: 'I believe I'm parked legally. If you'll excuse me, I'm calling on a friend.'

I locked Bile and went to her door. They followed, waited behind as I kept my finger on the bell...

'Who is it?'

'It's me, Chris.'

A bolt was pulled and the door opened. She was in a dressing-gown, framed in the light.

'I'm sorry, Sally, but I've been evicted–'

'Do you know this man, miss?'

'Of course I do–'

'Can I sleep on your sofa, or something, just for tonight, otherwise I've got to be–'

'You're under no obligation, miss.'

'I know that,' she said sharply. 'Come in, Chris, of course you can stay. Will there be anything else, Officers?' she demanded coldly.

'No,' muttered Jim, and she closed the door.

'I can't understand it,' she said later, after I'd told her what had happened. 'The police just aren't like that in Oxford.'

My brain had begun to function again after a second cup of coffee. 'They've been got at.'

'Oh, rubbish.'

I repeated what Jim's friend had said about being told to make sure I was out of the county.

'Well, maybe,' she said reluctantly, 'but who?'

'Phil.'

'Now that *is* ridiculous. Why should–'

'Listen.' I leaned forward. 'Don't you remember how he kept on at me at lunchtime until I told him where I was staying?'

'Well, yes, but–'

'It can't be a coincidence, can it? Does he have any police connections?'

'Not as far as I know.' She paused. 'But Ron has. He's a Mason, and there are always high-ranking police in the Masons, aren't there?'

'Phil told him, then.'

'But *why*, Chris? It doesn't make sense. Why should they want you to leave so badly?'

'John.' I looked up. 'It's got to be to do with John and his AIDS work. You remember you told me last night you thought he'd hidden his data in the computer?'

'Yes?'

'Well, you were right.' I told her how I'd found part of it and how Dave had twice threatened me. 'You're sure you've no idea where Dave came from? Who brought him to the lab? Carey?'

'No, it was Ron, he–'

'Ron! Maybe that's the connection.' I told her how Ron had tried to make me leave that morning.

She put her hand to her head. 'No wonder

119

you wanted to speak to me, I'm sorry I put you off. Chris, I think you've got to go to the police about his. Oh–' she got up from her chair, came and sat beside me on the settee and put a hand on my arm – 'don't worry, I'll come with you. We'll get that doctor to come as well, they'll have to listen then.'

I hesitated. 'All right.'

'You're not thinking of running away, are you? Sorry, I shouldn't have said that. I'd be scared in your position.'

'I had been thinking of running,' I said, not looking at her. 'The truth is, I'm a bit of a coward. That Dave–' I found her eyes – 'he really does scare me.'

She touched my arm again. 'You're not a coward, Chris, anyone would be scared by Dave. He scares me, too.' She gripped my hand impulsively. 'What I really find so hard to take is that so many people could be involved.'

'Yes. Did Phil say anything about me this evening?'

'I'd rather hoped you'd forgotten that,' she said, releasing me. 'No, he didn't.'

'Sure?'

'Quite sure.'

There was a silence, then she said, 'I know what you're thinking: why did I go out with him again after what I'd said?'

I shrugged. 'Your business.'

'Well, if you must know, we had a bit of a scene.' I said nothing. 'He made it plain that he wanted more than I could offer, so I told him what I should have told him in the first place. That we could only be good friends.'

Another silence.

'And he didn't like that?' I said at last.

'No.' She studied her hands. 'He – he kept bringing your name up.'

'So he did mention me, then?'

She raised her eyes. 'I suppose he did.'

I slowly smiled. 'Lucky that *we're* just good friends, isn't it?'

She smiled back. 'Yes.'

Our faces moved closer, tilted, our lips just brushed at first, then we kissed harder as our arms stole about each other.

'Well, this is a turn-up,' she said breathlessly, a few minutes later.

'Is it?'

'No,' she said softly, 'not really.'

'I've always wanted you,' I said.

'Then why didn't you…?'

'John.' I looked down. 'And Jill.'

She took my hand and gently stroked it, lifted it to her lips, then, with her eyes fast on mine, she closed it round her breast.

CHAPTER 7

There was almost no reaction to my appearance at work the next morning; Ron grunted, Phil and Carey both ignored me and Dave wasn't there. Sally and I had come in separately, she on her bike and me in Bile.

I spent the morning cocooned in the glow from the night, savouring every sensation, every scent, touch and endearment... I hadn't realized how much I needed her, or was it just that I'd needed a woman? I don't know. I don't think I was in love with her then.

The next surprise came at coffee-time. Everyone was sitting round in silence as usual, when Ron said, 'I suppose I ought to mention, for those who are interested, that Mr Devlin has at last had the grace to contact me.'

Half a dozen heads came up, mine included. John had rather slipped from my mind.

'Apparently, he went to visit his mother in

Glasgow, then went down with summer 'flu.'

'Did he say when he'd be back?'

'He said he'd try and come back by the end of next week. I'll say this, he sounded pretty rough – I hardly recognized him.'

As I sat back, I realized my relief was twofold. Now that I knew he was all right, I wasn't in such a hurry to see him.

Immediately after coffee, Ron called Ian and me into his office.

'Have you got that mess in the cell-culture lab sorted out yet?'

'It's not a problem any more,' said Ian. 'Not now that Val's back and we know John won't be here.'

'Well, I want you to handle the Special Clinic today and tomorrow. All right? You can start now.'

Outside the office, we looked at each other. Ian made a face.

'Ours not to reason why, I suppose,' he said.

The term 'special clinic', a euphemism for VD Clinic, is now itself an anachronism, since it prefers to be known as the Department of Genito-Urinary Medicine.

Some venereal diseases can be diagnosed microscopically on the spot, enabling the venereologist to prescribe a treatment immediately, which is very useful, since many of the patients simply don't come back. Thus the need for a small laboratory on-site.

It's not particularly demanding work; a nurse brings through a specimen and waits while it's cultured and examined under the microscope.

'Business is booming more than ever,' Ian told me cheerfully as we walked over. 'It's AIDS, of course. So many people want tests that they're open six days a week now.'

'Don't they set aside times for the AIDS people?'

'Sure, but they don't turn them away at other times, otherwise they'd only go and donate a pint of blood to get the test done, and risk passing on the virus that way.'

It happened about half way through the afternoon. The laboratory was a small, enclosed area off one of the consulting rooms, and within easy reach of the other two. Ian was flirting with one of the nurses, who was young and pretty, while I was at the microscope, searching for Gonococci.

'Oh no! No!' A woman's voice from the adjoining room – we all looked at each other.

Then there was a scream and a crash as something hit the floor.

The nurse pulled open the door and leapt to the aid of a colleague struggling with a woman of about thirty, who was still emitting gurgled screams.

'D'you think we should help?' asked Ian in an undertone.

'No. They know what they're doing.'

Already they had the woman in a chair, where they pulled up her sleeve and administered a sedative.

The door behind us opened and one of the other consultants looked in.

'What's going on?'

'Patient got hysterical,' I said. 'Seems to be under control now.'

'Thank God for that! Better get back to mine before they go the same way.'

As he withdrew his head, the nurse came back.

'Are you all right?' said Ian.

'Yes, thanks.' Her voice shook and her hair was dishevelled. 'We'll get her over to Casualty in a minute. Have to bring her through here so as not to alarm the other patients.'

'What was it?' I asked quietly.

'Can't you guess? She's just been told she's got the AIDS virus.'

I thought about that for the rest of the afternoon. It brought it home to me more than anything else could that John's discovery meant more than kudos for him, or Carey's pride, or profits for firms like Parc-Reed.

Sally and I stayed in that night. In fact, as soon as I got back (she was there before me) we wordlessly went to her room and spent an hour or so rediscovering each other. Then, after a quick meal, went back to bed in case we'd missed anything.

On Friday morning Ron called me to his room and told me that since they were still short-staffed, I could stay on for the time being, provided I worked exclusively at the clinic. It was tempting to prod him about why he'd changed his mind, but I decided not to risk it.

As I walked over to the clinic, Dave fell into step beside me. I hadn't known he was back and nearly levitated with the shock.

'So you're staying on for a while, then?'

'That's right,' I replied, trying to control my voice.

'I'm going to find Devlin's data one way or another.' He paused. 'Perhaps we could do a deal.'

'I don't know what you're talking about,' I said. Suddenly, I wasn't so frightened of him.

'I'd think about it if I were you. Seriously. You can always find me–'

'I still don't know what you're talking about.' I stopped and faced him. 'You must speak to him about it when he comes back.'

His eyes narrowed but he didn't try to follow me as I walked away.

I saw him again that evening. Sally and I were at Brown's, a large eating house apparently peculiar to Oxford and Cambridge. Not surprisingly, a lot of the customers are students, but the food is good and cheap and the atmosphere cosmopolitan and heady.

Sally suddenly looked past my shoulder. 'Isn't that Dave over there?'

I turned in my seat. He was leaning against the bar, watching us. Sally waved and he raised a hand in reply.

'This is getting farcical,' I said, and told her what had happened that morning.

'You know what it is,' she said, looking at me. 'He thinks you're in touch with John.'

'D'you know, I think you're right. The stupid thing is that I couldn't help him find John's data, even if I wanted to.'

'I could.' Her eyes were fast on my face. 'I bet I could work out his password.'

'How?'

'Because I know him, I know how his mind works.'

'Go on, then.'

At that moment, a waitress came up and asked whether we'd like to see the menu again.

'Yes, please,' said Sally, then to me, 'later. First things first.'

We didn't talk about it again until the next evening, Saturday. We'd spent the morning in bed and the afternoon in a punt on the Cherwell, in the gloriously unreal world above Magdalen Bridge of sunlight and hanging leaves, tree roots dipping into dark green shadows, and laughter, sharp on the water. In the centre of a city and yet miles from anywhere.

'Knowing John,' she said that evening over her second drink, 'and I do know John, he's chosen something so obvious that we'll kick ourselves when he tells us.'

'What sort of thing?'

'Oh, something that's staring us in the face.' She leaned on her elbows. 'If it's not an anagram of his name, it'll be something egotistical, something he thinks reflects his own cleverness.'

'Well, I've tried everything I could think of.' I listed them.

She shook her head. 'Nowhere near. Let's try some anagrams.'

She pulled out a pad and we tried for an hour without much success.

'I'll get it eventually,' she said, putting the pad away.

I awoke in the morning to find her tickling my stomach. Grey eyes watched mischievously through gold hair. Her hand moved.

'You'll be lucky,' I growled sleepily.

But she was. She was irresistible, and afterwards I fell back into a deep sleep.

The telephone was ringing.

'Answer it for God's sake,' I mumbled, reaching over.

The other side of the bed was empty and I woke with a start.

No sign of her. I leapt out of bed and snatched the 'phone.

'Er – hello?'

A chuckle. 'Thought that would get you up.' Sally.

'Where are you? You had me worried.'

'I've found it,' she said softly.

'Found what?'

'The password, silly. Staring us in the face, like I said.'

'Are you at the lab?'

'No, John's flat.'

'What about Mr Thing?'

'Singh. Still in bed, I expect.'

'Well, don't keep me in suspense. What is it?'

'Come on over and I'll show you.'

'Don't be daft, we'll be caught. Come back here, and we'll go to the lab and try it.'

She chuckled again. 'No, you come over here.' There was a clunk as she disconnected.

With a sigh, I pulled on some clothes and set off. The streets were deserted, except for a few people in their Sunday best.

The front door wasn't locked. I gently pushed it open and peered into the gloom, then crept upstairs.

John's door was ajar. When is a door not a door? Chorus: When it's a jar!

She must have heard me coming because she was pretending to be asleep. John's briefcase lay open beside her.

I picked up a piece of Parc-Reed notepaper. 'It's Prince Charming,' I said, leaning over her; then I saw the marks on her neck.

Touched her shoulder. Pulled her over and

her lifeless grey eyes stared past me.

Don't know how long I stood there, staring. I knew she was dead, which is why I didn't try... A noise behind me, a crash...

All I could see was the carpet, stretching away like a plain under the bed. It was dusty. There was a pair of shoes.

I thought without thinking about it that I must have fainted, my cheeks seemed to be glued by saliva to the rough carpet, my neck hurt...

Perhaps it wasn't true! I dragged myself up – she was still there and–

My eyes bolted and I turned and heaved on to the carpet.

She was now naked from the waist down!

I'm going mad, they said I would– No! No, I'm not ... get out, find police.

Drew a sleeve over my mouth and ran for the door.

Weasel-face peering across the landing, eyes grotesque behind lenses...

'Don't go in there!' I shouted, stumbled down the stairs, along the hall, pulled the door–

A huge figure blotted out the light.

'Oh my God!' I clutched blue material. 'Up there, she's up there. Go and look if you don't believe me.'

He stared, then there was a cry from up-stairs and he turned.

'Cop hold of matey here, while I take a look.'

He moved past me and another hand, gentle but firm, gripped my arm.

Flies were buzzing round my face – no, specks of dust, going faster–

Then I was sitting on the cold wall of the pathway, head between knees, someone's hand on my neck.

It hurt...

'Go and radio a couple more cars, quick. I'll look after sunshine here.'

I was pulled to my feet. I said, 'You've got to get after him,' and started for the gate.

'Oh no you don't!'

My arms were pinioned and cold steel clamped my wrists.

I turned in amazement. 'You don't think it was me, do you?'

He gazed impassively. 'What I think doesn't matter, but we'll be wanting you to help us with our inquiries. Down at the station.'

His companion came back. 'They're on their way.' He looked at me curiously, then back to the other. 'Dead?'

'Strangled by the look of it. After sexual assault.'

Weasel-face emerged, pointed at me. ''E dun it, Officer, I saw 'im. 'E dun it all right.'

A knot of people gathered by the gate.

'Better get sunshine into the car.'

'Move along there, please.'

Part of me was thinking: I never thought they really said that.

My thoughts were cut off by the hee-hawing of police cars.

More police, emerging from nowhere.

'Where is it?'

'Up there.'

'Anyone told Forensic yet?'

''E dun it, I saw 'im!'

'Get a statement from that man.'

'Better get this one down to the station.'

'Cautioned him yet?'

'You're under arrest. You're not obliged to say anything, but if you do say anything...'

Houses streaming by and the mad donkey-bray of the car's siren, my thoughts in tune with it: Not true ... not true ... not true...

CHAPTER 8

I think I had them wondering at first. I told my story simply and calmly and although the questions became harder and more oblique as the day wore on, they didn't shake me.

After that, I saw a solicitor. He was about my age and called Henry. Solicitors aren't paid to believe their clients, but I could see that Henry believed me. He asked if he could speak to my previous employers in Somerset and my GP and I told him he could do anything, if it helped. By the time he left, I had begun to hope.

That all changed the next day. By then, Ron and Phil and Singh and Weasel-face had had their say.

'You didn't have a "romantic" relationship with Miss Wytham at all, did you, Randall?' My tormentor had steel-blue eyes in a craggy face and called himself Inspector Johnson. 'The truth is, she put you up for a night out of pity, and then couldn't get rid of you. Imposed yourself on her, didn't you?'

The room was bare save for a tin ashtray on the stained table between us. A uniformed officer sat to one side, writing.

I tried to keep calm. 'That's not true. She was glad to put me up the night your officers moved me on, as they themselves witnessed–'

'But she didn't invite you to move in permanently, which is what you did.'

A little daylight was trying to squeeze through the high window, past the fluorescent strip that provided most of the light.

'As a matter of fact, that's just what she did–'

'Listen, Randall–' he leaned forward – 'we've got a witness, a colleague and close friend of Miss Wytham, who quotes her as saying that she was sick of you, that you imposed yourself on her, that she just wanted to be rid of you.'

'That's a lie!' I shouted. 'Who is this–'

'And we've got another witness–'

'It's Philip Snow, isn't it?'

Johnson raised his voice, but otherwise carried on as though I hadn't spoken – 'your boss, who says that at work, you wouldn't leave Miss Wytham alone, you persisted in forcing your attentions on her. He says that he had to speak to you about it last Wednesday and suggested that you leave, but that you were most reluctant to accept–'

'That's not true, he changed–'

'Well, he's your boss and that's what he says. And on top of that, we've got a witness who as good as saw you kill her.'

'Weasel-face! You don't believe him, surely?'

'Mr Albert Sims, you mean? Why shouldn't I believe him?' He opened the folder in front of him and found the relevant statement. 'He heard raised voices, a quarrel, then a woman screaming. Then he heard, and I quote, "Thumps and bangings. Then everything went quiet for a bit, I don't know exactly how long. Then there were more noises. After a bit, I looked out, and as I did, the man I now know to be Randall came out. He looked very excited and shouted at me, 'Don't go in there,' then he ran down the stairs. I could see what looked like a body on the bed."' Johnson looked up.

I said, 'He didn't see me do it.'

'Just missed you, didn't he?'

'No, because I didn't–'

He smashed his fist into the table and the ashtray jumped. 'Come *off* it, Randall! You're not fooling anyone.' He flicked a page. 'Another witness, the landlord, saw Miss Wytham arrive, and then a short while later, you. This bothered him, because a few days previously, he had found both of you together in the flat. I quote: "Miss Wytham was looking worried and tried to make Randall leave. He didn't want to go, and when she persuaded him, he tried to steal a briefcase belonging to the rightful tenant."'

'I've already explained–'

'And this morning we've had some preliminary forensic evidence. The semen found in Miss Wytham is of your blood group and tissue type, and we've sent it for DNA fingerprinting–'

'It would be the same since I'd made love with her that morning.'

'I wouldn't call what you did making love. Tell me this, Randall: if you didn't kill her, who did?'

'I don't *know*–'

'No one else was seen entering the house, just Miss Wytham, then you. You followed her there, didn't you, Randall?'

'No, she 'phoned–'

'She was trying to get away from you, wasn't she?'

'No, I–'

'No one else was seen, Randall, no one.'

'Then there must be a back way out–'

'The back door was bolted from the

inside. Tell me, Randall, just out of interest, why did you run for it after your 999 call?'

'I wasn't running for it, I didn't make any call.'

'Yes, you did, I have the text here.' He looked down. '"Please come quickly, I think I've killed her."'

'I didn't make that call.'

'The receiver was still off the hook when we got there, that's how we managed to trace it.'

'It wasn't me.'

'Your whole story is fantastic. What about this?' He found my statement. '"I remember waking up on the floor. I must have been hit from behind, because when I stood up, I found Miss Wytham half undressed, which she hadn't been before..." You expect us to believe that?'

'It's the truth,' I said tiredly.

'But where's the evidence? You have slight bruising to the side of your head and neck, which could have come from anywhere, perhaps when you fainted.'

He leaned forward again. 'You see, Mr Randall, I *am* prepared to believe that you fainted. In fact, I'm prepared to believe that you genuinely can't remember much about it. That in effect you *did* recover from a faint and find Miss Wytham in the way you describe. And because you couldn't believe that *you'd* done it, why then, it must be someone else.'

He leaned back. 'We might even be talking about manslaughter. With your background, I should think that's quite possible. Better than murder, isn't it?'

'I didn't do it,' I said slowly and carefully. 'I'm not mad, or deranged, I just didn't–'

'Who said anything about being mad?' he cut in swiftly.

'You did, just now, you said–'

'*I* didn't say anything about being mad or … what was it? Deranged? Those were *your* words, Mr Randall.'

'Well, I'm not either of them.'

'*I* didn't say you were.' A heavy silence. Then: 'Think about it, Mr Randall.' A pause, 'Now…' And so we went back to the beginning, but from a different angle as he probed and prodded for weaknesses.

Hours later, my cell seemed like a haven, almost a homecoming. The bars swung shut and the keys jingled – fine, if it meant getting away from Johnson for a while.

Oh, Sally … but my mind couldn't grasp what had happened to her.

Homecoming… God, what wouldn't I

give to see the inside of my cottage now? My throat swelled as I sank on to the hard bed and thought about what it looked like, felt and smelt like…

A little later Henry called and I was very glad to see him, but as I told him about my interrogation, his face told me that something was wrong.

When I'd finished, he said, 'I've had a chance to look at all the statements now, and I've also spoken to your doctor.' He took a breath. 'Quite honestly, if the police are offering to reduce the charge to manslaughter, I think it's something we must consider.'

I gaped at him. 'But I didn't do it. Admitting manslaughter is saying I did.'

He took off his glasses. 'I must tell you quite frankly, Mr Randall, that if you insist in pleading Not Guilty, I don't rate your chances very highly.'

'Are you saying you think I did it?'

'What I think doesn't matter. What matters from now on is the evidence, and there's a great weight of it against you. You realize you're going to be charged tomorrow, don't you?'

I could only shake my head.

'Listen.' He leaned forward. 'Not only is manslaughter preferable to murder, but now that I know your background and medical history, I'm almost certain that you could get a reduced sentence on the grounds of diminished responsibility, especially if we can get the psychiatrist who saw you to give evidence for you.'

'But I didn't–'

'Think about it very seriously, Mr Randall. Now, do you want me to be present when you're charged?'

My head sank into my hands. 'Will it make any difference?'

'I was thinking of moral support. It's up to you.'

Homecoming. My cell didn't seem so much of a haven now – there'd be letters at home, waiting to be opened…

Suddenly I realized I might never see them … what was life imprisonment now? Ten years? And to think I'd thought it too little… I buried my face in the pillow and felt myself spiral down, down into blackness.

Prison. Three to a cell. Filth. Sodomy. AIDS. All inevitable.

My body shook with sobs, convulsed, then suddenly stopped.

I sat up. There was complete silence.

I'd rather die now, rather kill myself. I'm

no use to anyone.

How?

No knives here, only plastic cutlery with meals.

Hang myself, that's the traditional way. I looked around the cell, where could I...?

The window-bars, maybe I could... I rose, went over to them. Reached up, touched them.

I recoiled as though they were electrified, sank on to my bed and trembled. *I'd really meant it.*

Can't give in ... suicide ultimate surrender...

Now I wanted to scream, hurl myself at the bars, *make* them understand, *make* them let me out...

But I was in no position to make anyone do anything.

Very slowly I became calmer, and thought. Thought about the evidence.

It was true I'd seen a psychiatrist. It happened about a month after I'd killed Jill. Liz, her sister, used to come and see me, see how I was. We'd always got on.

That evening, we were sitting down together. I held her hand. Put an arm round her. Kissed her.

She'd let me at first, then stiffened as she'd

realized what I wanted.

'It won't bring her back, Chris,' she'd said quietly.

'I know. Please, I need you.'

It was true. I had to have a woman, now, make sure I was all still there.

'Please!'

She'd stood up. I grabbed at her, tried to kiss her again, then a ringing slap sent me back on my heels.

She hadn't run away, which was something, I suppose, but she said it was as though I'd been another person. She made me promise to see a psychiatrist.

I did. He told me there was nothing wrong with me, but they always say that, don't they? He'd suggested I find a woman who was willing.

So how d'you get from there to being mad?

Because Johnson knows ... he wouldn't have spoken like that ... would he?

What if the psychiatrist now says I *am* deranged? What if I really am mad?

What if I really had killed Sally?

My head reeled and I fell back against the cold white tiles that lined the cell. God! Why don't they still hang people like me?

I wanted to jump up and confess.

No!

No, I'm not mad.

I went over what had happened again – no, it's all right, I didn't kill her. Whatever they do to me, *I* know that.

Johnson again, the following morning. 'Just want to check over a few details.'

'I want to make a statement,' I said.

He considered me for a moment, then told me to go ahead.

'The flat Sally was killed in belongs to John Devlin, Sally's boyfriend – *ex*-boyfriend. As I told you before, he's also a friend of mine. He works at the National Microbiology Lab too, but he's away at the moment.'

'Well?'

'Well, he told me a few months ago that he was working on a cure for AIDS.'

Johnson stared back blankly.

'You'd agree that that could be worth something?'

'Go on.'

'He'd hidden his data in the lab computer – you need a special password to get into the program. Well, Sally and I were looking for that password.'

'Why?'

'Because so many other people also

seemed to be looking for it.'

'Who, for instance?'

'Wait a minute. Sally did find the password, that morning in John's flat. She 'phoned me and–'

'Did she tell you what it was?'

'No, she told me to come round, which I did. And when I got there–' I swallowed – 'she was dead.'

'And fully dressed, I believe you said.'

'Yes.'

'And then you were knocked out, and when you recovered, she was undressed?'

'Don't you see?' I shouted. 'Whoever killed her was looking for that password as well. They want John's discovery.'

'And who might this person be?'

I leaned forward. 'He's called Dave. I don't know his surname, but he also works at the laboratory.' I told them as much as I could remember about him.

'And so this Dave,' said Johnson, 'you're saying he was in the flat as well?'

'Obviously.'

'And he hit you, undressed Miss Wytham and then dialled 999?'

'Yes,' I said defiantly.

'And then vanished without anyone seeing him go in or out, although they did see Miss

Wytham and they did see you.'

'It's what happened,' I said, burying my face in my hands.

To be fair, Henry told me later that the police went to the laboratory and asked about John. They were told that he was off sick but expected back at the end of the week, and no, he certainly wasn't working on a cure for AIDS. They also interviewed Dave and eliminated him from their inquiries.

I was glad Henry was with me when I was charged, even if he didn't believe me.

'Christopher Randall, you are charged that on the 22nd May 198-, you did murder Sally Wytham...' The words, spoken in formal, almost religious, tones – but it's you, *you,* they're talking to...

Then in a dream to a specially convened Magistrates' Court, where I was remanded in custody for a week. Then Oxford Prison, where my body and, in a clear plastic bag, my belongings, were officially handed over to the prison authorities.

I spent the night alone in a cell. It was more luxurious than the police cell, not that that mattered. The light was left on and I was regularly checked, or so the noise from the Judas flap indicated. Then in the morning, handcuffed between two prison offi-cers, I was driven to Winchester Prison.

In quick succession, I was taken to the Governor, Doctor and Chaplain, but can't remember anything they said. Then I was put in a cell with a grey-haired child molester called Charlie, 'to stop me doing anything foolish', as he explained to me.

Actually, Charlie wasn't so bad. At first, I ignored him and he simply shrugged and waited. When I did want to talk, he listened, and after a few days, he seemed almost normal. But then, so did I to him, perhaps.

I spent my time in a daze.

If I thought about Sally, opened my imagination to what had happened to her, I would experience a moment's unbearable grief and curl up like a fœtus on my bed, then my mind would shut off. So I stopped thinking about her. Perhaps the mind can only take so much.

One night I woke up knowing that John must be dead as well. Dave had killed them both. And something else came to me, un-bidden and irrelevant. The password.

Porridge. The exercise yard under the blue sky and achingly white cumulus. Meals. The screws, sometimes jocular, sometimes not, but always in charge. The clang of the door, the rattle of the Judas flap. Lights out. Charlie playing with himself.

CHAPTER 9

On Saturday I had a visitor, Jill's brother Alan. I was surprised, because although we'd got on well enough, we weren't that close. Perhaps he came out of a sense of duty.

He was acutely embarrassed, his eyes kept darting around and the chair creaked under his weight. After ascertaining I had no immediate needs, he couldn't think of anything else to say.

'How's Alison?' I asked.

'Fine, thanks.'

'And the kids?'

'Terrific.' He smiled, his eyes still for a moment.

'How long have you got this time?'

'Nearly a week. Sailing from Avonmouth on Wednesday.' Alan's a captain in the Merchant Navy.

'Good of you to spare the time to come and see me.'

'Oh, that's all right,' he replied awkwardly. 'No trouble.'

'Where are you going this time?'

'Same as usual. Portugal.'

'I envy you.'

'Nothing to be envious of. Never stay long enough to get to know...' He tailed off as he realized the significance of my remark. 'Sure there's nothing else you need?'

Twenty minutes later I was back in my cell with Charlie. Well, it had made a change.

On Tuesday I was taken back to Oxford to be re-remanded. I didn't really think they'd give me bail, but you never know, so I went.

There were four of us in the taxi, the driver, two screws and me between them, handcuffed to the one on my right.

It took about twenty minutes to get through the city (girls in summer frocks and women pushing prams, free, all of them) and on to the A34. Although the traffic was heavy, we kept up a pretty good speed, 60 or 70 in the outside lane, overhauling the lines of heavy lorries on their way to the Midlands.

Nobody spoke much.

I looked down at the cuff around my right wrist. It was a solid, square affair, more complex than the police ones. I moved my hand slightly. It wasn't tight, and I wondered whether, if left to myself, I could pull it through. Some hope!

I looked out. Didcot power station loomed ethereally through the summer haze, water-vapour rising lazily into the sky from the six huge cooling towers. I remembered hearing about a glider pilot on a record distance attempt using them as a thermal to–

A bang like a gun going off, and the articulated lorry overtaking on the other carriageway slewed towards us. In slow motion, it burst through the barrier on the central reservation ... our driver shouted, tried to sheer away, but there was another lorry on his left...

The artic hung over us, I remember watching its offside tyre shredding like paper, then it smashed into the back of us. We spun underneath the trailer. Darkness. Another smash as the roof caved in and we were dragged along sideways, prevented from overturning by the trailer wheels, metal screeching in agony as it tore apart–

Stillness and absolute silence.

Horns blasting and tyres screaming.

I felt as though I'd been hanged, head nearly torn from my body. Voices like a dream. Then:

'Jesus Christ! Jack! Jack, can you hear me?'

The driver was dead, eyes staring from an impossible angle. Jack, the screw on my left, was unconscious, maybe…

The officer on my right started attacking the door with his free hand, then leaned against me and drew back his feet … it burst open.

'Come on, matey.' He wriggled out, pulling me after him, then led me between the wrecked cars (one or two people struggling out) and on to the grass verge.

He looked around. Another crash-barrier ran behind it. He gave a grunt of satisfaction, found the key and unlocked his cuff. Then before I realized what he was doing, he turned my back to the barrier, wrenched my left arm over, my right under it, and locked the cuff on my left wrist.

'That should hold you,' he muttered, and ran back among the crashed cars.

'Hey!' I shouted. 'You can't leave me here!' But he'd gone.

I gazed around at the litter of vehicles. People stumbled about, some dazed, some trying to help.

Already, my back ached. I could neither sit nor stand and the barrier, pressing into me, forced my back into an arch.

I pulled at my hands, trying to find a more comfortable–

The right cuff, still loose!

I looked for the screw. No sign of him. I pulled hard and the cuff dug into the base of my palm, harder, *harder* ... no good.

The angle was wrong, twist it round, try again.

I heaved.

It wouldn't budge ... *but the barrier did!*

I studied it. It was old and rusty, and to my left it disappeared into a clump of nettles. I couldn't see where it ended, but perhaps...

No one seemed to be aware of me. I began to edge along on bent knees. My foot slipped and I fell back ... didn't cry out, forced myself up again and along, legs moving like a crab, kneecaps screaming...

I peered into the nettles ... yes, it was bolted on to an upright stake.

I pulled again, and it shifted, grated.

I moved into the nettles, trying to kick them down, felt them stroking my hands, the sudden bite as they stung. Go *on*...

Reached the stake. It was rotten and the bolt holding the barrier in place was loose.

I took a breath and heaved, felt the wood crumble as the bolt pulled through ... but not enough. Pulled harder. No good.

In desperation, I lifted a foot and kicked back, felt the wood cracking ... and the bolt coming free.

Now ... down on my knees ... along till I feel the bolt ... push my hands, arms, back into the nettles, trying to get them round...

A scratch of metal to metal. Further, go further–

I fell forward on to my face as my hands came free, then shakily got to my feet.

A man was staring at me, puzzled.

I turned, stepped awkwardly round the barrier – he'd see the cuffs now, can't help that – through more nettles, then toppled over the edge of a bank and slid down, like a sledge.

I saw the brambles just in time and rolled into a ball.

They gripped my jacket and trousers as I pulled myself upright and tore free. Ducked through a wooden fence and fell into a ditch.

It was dry, soft with new grass, and I just lay there for a moment, breath sobbing.

Then sat up. The ditch ran straight and clear, both ways.

I pulled at the handcuffs again. No good. It might be different if they were in front of me–

In front.

I raised myself on my knees and bent forward, trying to force my hands under my backside... Not quite: my jacket pulled under my armpits.

Up again, crouch, force hands under buttocks, pull, pull, and *bend!*

Shoulder-sockets bursting, my hands came to rest on my thighs.

Tried to pull my feet through – heels in the way. Kicked off my shoes, lay on my side and, one at a time, my feet squeezed through.

I lay gasping for a moment, then looked at my hands. They were covered in angry red weals–

Have they missed me yet?

I pulled on my shoes, stood up and started running. North.

Needed to get to the other side of the road, but how? Daren't climb the bank–

I tripped on a stone and fell, but my outstretched hands took the force. On and on, along the bottom of the ditch. Then I found it.

A drainage tunnel, a hollow tube of concrete beneath the road. A circle of light at the far end. I scrambled in.

The cuffs made crawling almost impossible. If only...

They're in front now. Try again.

I sat against the concrete and forced the ball of my right thumb into my palm, and with the left hand, pushed... It wouldn't quite go, not quite...

Put my hand down, placed my shoes either side and pulled, shoved with my feet...

Slowly, like toothpaste, my hand squeezed through.

I massaged it for a few moments, then started crawling. The cuffs, dangling from my wrist, jingled like Christmas bells on the concrete... They must have missed me by now... Keep going.

The hole of daylight grew bigger suddenly. I fell through it and the sun beat my face. Which way?

North. I knew where I was going now. Another ditch, muddier this time.

I ran. How far to the road? A mile? Then how far to Didcot Station?

The ditch grew shallower, ceased. I was beside a cornfield. The ground was easier, but also, I could be more easily seen.

Cars brushed by overhead. Keep going.

Must have missed me by now. Keep going.

Jog, jog, my innards jiggled up and down like blancmange, my windpipe grew raw as I dragged in air. Keep going. Just keep going.

Then there was a fence ahead. Bushes, and a garage.

Steal a car? No, not a hope, have to try and thumb–

No, they'll have the police cars out soon … but if I lie low, the dogs will find me…

I ducked through the fence, skirted the garage and reached the road. Looked down – the cuffs! Stuffed them into my jacket pocket.

My trousers and shoes were filthy, but my jacket wasn't too bad, except at the elbows. And I was wearing that badge of respectability, a tie, put on especially for the magistrates. I limped across the road and started walking, recovering my breath.

Always look back as you thumb; if the driver can see your face, he's more likely to stop. Lesson from student days. I looked back.

Cars passed monotonously.

Perhaps I should forget it and start running again. Could I run two or three miles? No, I'd be picked up before then – by the wrong people.

Cars, cars, grinding by. A driver gave me a V-sign, and you, you–

A blue Mini, woman driver, forget it. She sailed by, then miraculously checked, and stopped.

I ran. She was leaning across, opening the

door. Thin ascetic face, glasses. School-teacher.

'I'm only going as far as Didcot, but–' She broke off as she took in my filthy state.

I tried to smile. 'I – I apologize for my appearance.' Swallowed desperately. 'I was involved in the pile-up on the A34.' Genius! 'Perhaps you know about it?'

'No, I don't think...'

'I've got to get to London for a meeting, it's vital. Didcot'll do marvellously, I can catch a train, if you could just drop me at the station.'

She hesitated. 'All right.'

I eased in beside her and pulled the door shut with my right hand. The radio mumbled softly.

She pushed the car into gear, looked back and let in the clutch.

'Was anyone hurt?'

'A few. One seriously, I think. The police seemed to have everything under control.' Good, nice touch. If I could just get to Taunton–

'They didn't mind you leaving the scene, then?'

'Mmm?'

'The police.'

'No. They seemed glad to get people out

158

of the way.'

'Now you mention it, a police car did overtake me, going very fast.'

'Did you see any ambulances?'

She shook her head. 'No.' The cooling towers of the power station loomed over us. 'You weren't hurt at all, then?'

'Only cuts and scratches, as you can see.' Fine, fine.

The radio bleeped the time signal.

'Excuse me,' she said, 'I like to hear the news.'

My heart hit my throat – but they couldn't, not yet.

Round a roundabout. 'The Prime Minister said today...' Another roundabout. 'The latest round of disarmament talks...'

The station five hundred yards ahead. 'BBC Radio News at midday.'

I sagged with relief.

'A newsflash just in.' I closed my eyes, forced them open. 'Crash in Oxfordshire ... escaped prisoner ... wanted for murder ... five feet ten, well dressed ... do not approach.'

Silence.

Say something.

'You–' I coughed. 'You wouldn't happen to remember the times of the London trains, would you?'

Silence.

'Er – every hour, I think.' She knew.

A hundred yards.

'I'll pop in and check, then if there's time, slip over to that garage about my car.' Lies, as we both knew. 'I can't tell you how grateful I am.'

'It's – all right.'

She pulled into the station. I opened the door awkwardly, right hand again. 'Well, thanks very much.'

'It's all right.'

I didn't watch her go, just dived into the entrance hall.

It was an open station, thank God, no ticket collectors. I went up to the information board and tried to scan the blurry figures...

Thunder and a gentle vibration as a train from London came into the platform overhead.

I walked, almost ran, through the gate, right, up the stairs, emerged as the 125 slid to a halt.

'Didcot, this is Didcot. The train on Platform One is for Bristol Temple Meads only. Bristol Temple Meads only.'

Perhaps... How quickly would she get the

police? Where were the ticket inspectors, front or back? They were especially zealous now, with open stations.

A roar, as another train pulled in on the opposite platform for London. Good, it might confuse them.

Front or back?

I walked down the train. Doors were slamming.

Damn! First-class carriages. The whistle blew. Never mind, go in the loo. I ran to the back of the train and jumped on.

There was no loo. Too late to get off, the train was moving.

I waited until everyone had sat down, then walked through the carriage as fast as I could without running. Two or three pairs of eyes flickered from my shoes and trousers to my face.

Then I was through. Found the nearest cubicle and locked the door. Pulled down the seat cover and sat.

Reaction set in.

CHAPTER 10

I don't know how long I sat there, trembling uncontrollably, heart threshing against diaphragm. Can't remember how long it took before I could think again.

Had I done the right thing? My guilt would be confirmed in everyone's eyes now, but wasn't it anyway? I think I knew then what I had to do – if I could just remain free.

If. What were the statistics? Ninety per cent of escapees recaptured within three days? Something like that.

Concentrate on the present. My appearance. As I pulled my hand from my pocket, the cuff jingled. My hands throbbed.

Stood up and peered into the mirror – and peered. I simply didn't recognize the face that stared back. My hair was on end, my beard ragged, face covered in mud and scratches – all that – but it was the eyes. They stared back at me, wide and wild, with a fanatical glare.

I pulled out some paper towels, loosened my tie and cleaned up my face. Then took off my jacket, brushed off the worst of the mud and cleaned the elbows.

My trousers and shoes were worse than a tramp's. Shoes first. I washed them in the washbasin, pausing as the plughole became blocked with mud. Dried them.

Trousers. They were light brown and the mud showed up like chalk on a blackboard. I scraped at it with my comb, then washed off the rest – better to look wet than dirty. Then I plucked off the cotton threads snagged by the brambles, pulled them on and stepped into my shoes.

Mirror again – not too bad. I washed the comb and used it on my hair and beard, better still. Straightened my tie, and the dangling cuff flashed back at me – must do something–

There was a knock and the handle rattled up and down.

Swallowed. 'All right, I'm coming.' Last look round, hand in pocket, flick the catch–

A pair of reproachful eyes, female: 'About time too.'

'Sorry.' I slid past her – and into the arms of the ticket-collector.

'Oh! I beg your pardon.'

'That's all right, sir.'

I turned away. Had he heard the girl? The

door hissed aside. I could feel him following me. Not too fast now...

'Tickets, please.'

Not too fast, not too slow, half way, just keep walking...

'Tickets, please.'

Another hiss and I was through.

Both cubicles engaged. Wait or move on?

A click, one of the doors opened, and a man stepped out, with the sound of flushing.

Flushing! Must remember that next time. I locked the door and sat down.

Must stay long enough to let the inspector get well past.

How long before we reached Bristol? Thirty, forty minutes? Perhaps they'll think I caught the London train, or will they plan for both?

I took off my jacket and examined the handcuffs again. Found a handkerchief and tore a strip from it, then made two holes in my shirtsleeve with my teeth and tied the free cuff up with the strip. Replaced the jacket. Now at least I didn't have to have my hand in my pocket all the time.

What when I get to Bristol? Find a train for Taunton, there should be plenty.

Then what?

As soon as I tried to think beyond the next move, the enormity of it hit me and I began to tremble again.

One step at a time. Where was the collector? Give him a bit longer.

Why not stay here? No, someone'll notice.

How do I look now? Stood up, found the mirror. The scratches on my face showed, otherwise not too bad. Even the eyes seemed better – or was I just getting used to them?

Time to move. Checked myself over again for details, reached for the door–

You've forgotten to flush! Press down the pedal, surge of water.

Cautiously open door. Nobody. Peer through glass into carriage – there he was! Looking at the last few tickets, give him a minute or two…

'Excuse me!'

'Sorry.' Someone edged past. The door hissed.

I waited a couple of minutes, then walked easily through and locked myself into the next cubicle. Sat down.

Felt my right hand stealing over my left arm, feeling for the cuff.

How much longer – twenty, thirty minutes?

The compartment swayed to and fro as the wheels sang hollowly below. We were going fast, probably near the eponymous 125.

Found my hand feeling for the cuff again. Stood up, looked in the mirror, at the eyes that would stare out of tomorrow's papers, the eyes of a killer–

Jerked my head away, sat down.

Should I move again? The thought of the collector made my guts quail – I stood up abruptly, suddenly needing to urinate. It stung as it came out in hot spurts, splashing the seat and the lino floor.

Mopped it up with paper towels and sat down again. The lino was still shining wet and I felt sick.

Can't leave here, not again. What when we reach Bristol? Think, man, think!

No need to leave the station, just find the timetable and the platform for Taunton. Find the loo again.

When I got to Taunton, was it an open station? No, no – worry about that later, sufficient unto the *moment* is the evil thereof...

What are they doing at the crash site? For the first time, I thought about the dead driver and felt a surge of pity. Did he have a wife, children?

They'd hate me, blame me for his death. Everyone would hate me tomorrow, if I were still free. If...

Would the dogs have found my scent yet? Irrelevant. The woman in the car, so much depended on her. How near were the police, how long before she got them to listen to her? She'd be questioned, then they'd get on to British Rail to check the trains. I might have gone two – no, three ways – London, Bristol or Oxford. They'd have to arrange three receptions – if they believed her.

They'd believe her. So, would they be waiting in Bristol?

As though in answer, the brakes below squealed softly and the train's movements checked.

I swallowed, better get ready to go out – no!

No. If I went out now, I'd be forced on to the platform, better wait till nearly everyone has gone.

The brakes bit harder and the acrid smell of burnt lining rose into the cubicle. Noises as people pulled luggage from racks and the space outside the cubicle filled.

The rhythm of the wheels changed as the train lurched over some points, a jerk as the movement was checked further.

We entered the station. A window was pulled down and a door opened, not the one nearest the cubicle. People began moving out.

'All change!' blared the loud-speaker. 'All change!' The shuffling footsteps seemed to go on forever. How many people can you get on to a train?

I checked myself over, handcuff secure, hair tidy, shoes and trousers nearly dry – not that it matters, if they're here, they'll have my description. I stood paralysed for a moment by my heartbeat.

Less noise now… Try and look casual… I opened the door a crack and watched an old lady move slowly past. Slid out and peered down the gangway of the empty carriage, through the darkened windows–

The platform was crawling with police. One was looking intently through as he moved along the carriage – I ducked back. They'd be aboard any second!

Glanced back at the other door, there was another train alongside this one. I would be invisible from the other platform..

Without thinking, I pulled down the window, pushed the handle and slid the window back before gently lowering myself on to the oil-stained grit of the rail-bed between the trains. Pushed the door shut. Looked around. No faces, no one had seen me.

Which end would the driver of the other train be? No way of telling. I worked my way cautiously up the train I'd left. The police would be concentrating on the rear now.

Hot smell of oil and diesel fumes as I passed the idling motor, it was one of the three carriage units. I could see the end of it now, still no one in sight. Hovered behind the cab, still no one, got to risk it, plunged out in front of the cab, looked up to see a small boy staring solemnly down at me from the platform.

I raised a finger to my lips. 'I'm doing it for a bet. Come on, give us a hand up.'

I put elbows on the rough surface and pushed myself up, the boy pulling at my collar. The platform was littered with trolleys. Still no one had seen me.

I was nearly there when my sleeve slipped back and the handcuff glinted in the sun-light. I scrambled up, pulling the sleeve over it. Had he seen?

I ruffled his hair. 'Thanks. Our secret, eh?'

He gave a reluctant half-smile and ran off.

Hell! I looked round feverishly – better get lost in the crowd, look for a waiting-room. I moved between the trolleys, making for the stairs.

'Avonmouth…'

I stopped short, listening intently to the loudspeaker as it went through the list of stations again. 'Avonmouth, St Andrew's and Severn Beach – Platform Six.'

Alan, sailing tomorrow. Would he help? He'd bloody have to. Where the hell was platform six?

It seemed an age before I realized I was standing on it, that the train I'd crept around was the one I wanted.

A whistle blew. I turned, three strides, yanked open the door and jumped inside as it began to move. The springs in the seat pinged and groaned as I sank into them. The carriage was almost empty, just two old ladies with their backs to me, about ten yards away, gossiping.

I lowered my head as the platform slid past, wishing I had a newspaper to hide behind, then the train was pitching and swaying through an open space of sidings and weed-strewn ballast.

Ticket-collector, there was bound to be one, probably on his way now. Hard luck story? Even if it worked, I'd be remembered.

Hide under the seat? No, they were too open. Another loo? Too late now.

I looked behind me, at the empty seats – and the empty driver's cab.

Ahead again, still just the two old ladies, oblivious of me. Slowly rose to my feet –

more pings from the springs – and tiptoed back, five, six paces, through the sliding door and on to the driver's seat. A blind had been pulled down behind, presumably to stop people staring over his shoulder. I made sure it was secure and that I couldn't be seen through a crack.

The brakes squealed and the train lost speed. A station – I crouched down to avoid being seen by any passengers.

A door slammed, then another, and with a groan we were moving again, the train changing gear like a car.

'Fares, please!'

I jumped. Mumbled voices and the clink of change. Silence. Footsteps approaching. I squeezed behind the seat, no good, bound to be seen…

Closer … hard luck story … wallet pinched… Then, with a thump, the sliding door was drawn to and the footsteps receded. With closed eyes, I leaned back against the vibrating carriage wall.

The train slowed again and stopped. No passengers. I cautiously lifted my head as we pulled away, but couldn't see the name of the station.

The train lurched as we pulled off the main track on to a single line. A cutting. A station. A bridge over a main road. Another station, doors slamming, the boom and roar of a tunnel... How would I know when we reached Avonmouth?

Then sunlight flashed from a winding estuary, and with it, I felt a flash of hope.

More stations, estate houses, the estuary widening beneath the Avon bridge, and ahead a mess of factories, chimneys belching coloured smoke. Cranes – this must be it.

This time I waited a few seconds after the last slam, then stood up and fumbled with the door catch. It opened and I tumbled on to the platform. The train was moving–

'Hey!' The collector, leaning out of a window. I smiled and waved back as a couple of passengers looked round... The train didn't stop.

No one paid any more attention to me as I turned left into a street with shops. Just ahead was a small grassed area with some young trees and a bench. I walked over to it and sat down.

A faint breeze stirred the leaves overhead and cooled my face. I leaned back and closed my eyes, and slowly, very slowly, some of my nerve-endings began folding themselves back into place.

CHAPTER 11

Nearly an hour later I asked an old lady for the docks and she pointed to a gateway a couple of hundred yards down the road. I started walking.

I was nearly there, in fact I could see the bow of a ship, when a car swept past me. A policeman appeared from nowhere and flagged it down. The driver showed some sort of pass and was waved on.

Bloody hell! They must be dock police, but I daren't stop walking or suddenly turn round. Another car, the same thing happened, then I saw a turning on the right, just before the gate, and crossed the road to take it. Passed a huge Customs and Excise building, then a terrace of houses and offices.

At the end of the road was a children's playground overlooked by a housing estate. The docks lay behind a high wooden fence. I walked up to it. It was about eight feet high, made of stout posts sharpened at the top. Through it, I could see more ships.

I turned away and walked quickly through

the playground – better not be seen loitering here – and found a path parallel to the fence. Followed it.

Then came another terrace, wide, with ugly red brick houses and people leaning in doorways. At the end was another road, and another gate, marked Royal Edward Dock. A lorry was pounced on by the inevitable policeman.

How many docks were there? I walked a bit further, to some waste ground, but the wooden fence stretched as far as I could see.

My hair seemed to trap the sun's heat on to my head while the white pavement threw it up into my face. It was no good, I'd have to wait until dark and try and climb the fence. My tongue stuck to my mouth.

Where could I wait? There was nowhere, I hadn't the money even to sit in a café. Back to the bench under the trees, it was all there was. Perhaps find a loo with a tap.

I'd nearly reached the Customs and Excise house when a police car swept down the road from the station and stopped at the gate. A policeman got out and started showing something to the one at the gate.

I felt faint with sickness. Couldn't stop. Looked round in blind panic...

Steps beside me led up to a door. Beside it

was pinned a brass plate: 'Cairns and Pocock, Insurance Brokers'.

I turned without stopping and climbed the steps. Into a cool hall. Up a flight of stairs. On the landing, a door with a notice: 'Cairns and Pocock, next floor.' And underneath: 'Toilet.' I went in and locked the door.

It was narrow and dark. Pan at the end, under the window. Washbasin in front of me.

I turned on the cold tap and drank. And drank. Felt the cold water filling my belly like a balloon.

Then I started shaking again.

So near.

But was I?

Alan might turn me over to the police, they might be talking to him even now.

My head began to prickle. I sat on the edge of the seat and put it between my knees. Felt slightly better after a few minutes, but not much.

The water in my belly felt like mercury and my guts rumbled. Then, a warning, pricking sensation; I jumped up and got my trousers and pants down just in time.

After I'd cleaned myself up, I really did begin to feel better. If only I could stay here until dark ... unfortunately, lavatories aren't put into buildings for nothing, and sooner or later someone would want to use it.

The window immediately behind the pan was frosted, so I stood on the seat to get my bearings – *and found myself looking into the docks.*

I looked down. The ground was about fifteen feet below. Slowly raised my gaze. Sheds. Piles of pallets. Packing cases, cargoes, and beyond, cranes and ships.

I had to try it, even if it meant jumping.

Right, get the bottom window open. I got down and examined it. Probably hadn't been opened for years, but at least it wasn't sealed with paint.

I pushed back the catch, put my palms under the woodwork, and heaved.

It wouldn't budge. I straddled the pan and crouched, so as to use my legs. Heaved again.

Nothing. Then the door handle rattled.

I'd never have done it otherwise, but the shock somehow gave me strength, and with a crack, the window moved.

Trembling, I stopped and listened. Footsteps receding. Had they heard anything?

I turned back to the window. It moved reluctantly, groaning inch by inch. I pushed my head through.

A drainpipe! About a foot away, running down to ground level. I stuck out an arm and tried to shake it. It was solid.

I forced the window up another six inches, then took a breath and climbed on to the seat.

The locked door – if they break it in and find the window open, they'll inform the police.

Have to unlock it. But what if someone…?

Got to risk it.

I climbed down, listened, then unlocked it as gently as I could before darting back to the window.

No one in sight. He who hesitates…

I scrambled over the cistern, reached out, one hand on the pipe, then the other … my backside scraped over the ledge, drooped – then my legs fell into space. The pipe held and, hand over hand, I lowered myself until my feet hit the concrete below.

I walked away. No one in sight. I made for the high pile of pallets beside a corrugated iron shed and squeezed between them.

I looked back. No face at any window, although the one I'd come through grinned back at me like a broken tooth. Just some-one letting some air in.

What now? Look for the ship?

Too risky, police might still be there. Leave it till tomorrow morning.

My head began to prickle again and I knelt down. Could I stay here? No, it was too exposed. I forced myself to my feet and edged along the gap to the other side. It was all clear.

The shed had large double doors with a smaller door set in one of them. I tried it and to my relief, it opened.

Inside, it was hot and dirty and dimly lit by pencil beams of sunlight.

It was filled with builders' equipment, bricks, ladders, a cement mixer. I worked my way to the back. In one corner was a large heap of sacks. I looked at them for a moment, then gathered some up and made a bed behind a pile of breeze blocks.

I knew I wouldn't sleep, but just to lie down out of the glare of daylight, of eyes, that was enough. The sacks had an acrid smell and the air was warm and dusty.

Silence.

I pillowed my head on my arm and gradually, my heartbeat became slower.

CHAPTER 12

Bluebells dusted the floor of the wood and sunlight through the leaves lit Jill's coppery hair. We were following a path and I was telling her, quite naturally, all the things I'd ever felt about her.

'I know,' she said, and her smile embraced us both. She was there. She was real.

The wood changed into conifers and became dark and forbidding.

I shuddered, she touched my arm and said, 'It's going to be all right, Chris, really it is.'

I looked up to find Sally regarding me sombrely from a little way into the trees. She just nodded slowly.

I looked back at Jill, but she'd gone – they'd both gone. I threw myself down on the pine needles and wept.

The sackcloth rubbed against my wet cheek. It was pitch dark and I was cold. My bladder ached.

I couldn't find my way out, so I took a few cautious steps and relieved myself. Then I found some more sacks, pulled them over me and lay shivering.

Voices. A shaft of sunlight.

'Oh, great. I wonder what genius stacked 'em there.'

'C'mon, let's get on with it.'

Footsteps moved towards me. I looked round desperately, but there was nowhere to hide.

I stood up and the two men stopped dead. One tall, one short.

'What the bloody 'ell are you doin' 'ere?' said the taller.

What does a sailor sound like? I cleared my throat. 'Sorry, mate. Got pissed last night and couldn't find me ship. Kipped down 'ere.'

Their faces relaxed a little.

'You musta bin pissed, the ships are just over there.'

'Come over me sudden. Jus' 'ad to lie down.'

'What's your ship?'

'*Santiago*. Bound for Portugal.' Funny how these things come back to you.

'What's she carrying?'

'Steel.'

A grunt. 'I know her. You could be outa

luck, mate. She's due out this morning on the tide.'

'Oh Christ! Where is she?'

'Over in Royal Edward Dock.'

The other said, 'How come you didn't know that?'

''Cos I'm jus' joinin' her, that's why,' I said impatiently. 'Now how about showin' me the way?'

They looked at each other.

''E won't make it,' said the shorter.

'Unless...' said the taller.

'Shall we?'

'Why not?' He turned to me. 'C'mon, we'll take you over in the van.'

'Thanks.' I could hardly believe it. 'Sorry about this...'

'Never mind that now, c'mon.'

Feeling my left arm to make sure the cuff was secure, I followed them out into the morning sun, climbed into the battered old Transit and sat between them.

''Aven't you got a bag?' asked the shorter.

'Sent it on ahead.'

They seemed to accept this, and a moment later we were speeding across the greasy tarmac and past the line of ships I'd seen earlier. I sat silently, hoping they wouldn't think of any more questions, hoping I didn't smell – not that that really mattered.

We passed beneath the shadows of several huge warehouses, through an open area with rows of empty trailers, then over some sidings and into the other dock. I'd never have found it on my own.

'Gangplank's still down.'

'Looks like you're in luck,' said the taller.

The cranes beside the ship were still, and as we drew up I could see a couple of crewmen working in the stern. The name *Santiago* was streaked with rust.

'Thanks,' I said, meaning it.

They let me out, but stayed beside the van, watching as I approached the ship.

What if they wouldn't let me aboard? I mounted the gangplank. The two crewmen stopped work and one of them came towards me.

'You want something?' he said as I reached the top. Foreign accent, Portuguese, perhaps. 'We make sail. What you want?'

I smiled – raised a hand, for the benefit of the men below. 'Where's Captain Lydeard?'

'What you want him for?'

'Just take me to him. Very important.'

Reluctantly he said, 'Come,' and turned away. I waved at the men below and followed him up some steps to the bridge.

'God Almighty!' Alan's jaw dropped comically, or at least, it would have been if it wasn't so serious.

'Hello, Alan. Can we talk?'

'You want me to get rid of him, skipper?' said the crewman.

'No,' said Alan. 'Not yet, anyway, Leave us a few minutes.' The door clicked shut.

Alan turned on me. 'You must be bloody mad. I've got to give you up, you realize that, don't you.'

Statement, not question. How to play this?

'I'd give myself up, now, if I thought it would do any good. I didn't do it, Alan.'

'Just what am I suppose to say to that? God, man!' he exploded. '*I* could go to prison for this. Who the hell d'you think you are? What right have *you* got to risk *my* freedom?' He sighed. 'You wouldn't last a week in Portugal. Do you speak Portuguese? Have you got a passport? You'd be caught inside a few days, and I'd be done for helping you. Bloody *hell*, Chris—'

'I don't want to go to Portugal.'

Silence while he stared. Then:

'Where do you want to go?'

'Back to Oxford. Drop me off near Watchport. I'll swim if necessary.'

'Your house'll be watched. You'll be caught.'

'Let me worry about that.'

'But *why?* Why Oxford?'

'If I can get back, there's just a chance I can find something to prove my innocence. It's my only hope.'

Another silence. His eyes searched my face.

'You really mean that, don't you?'

'Yes. D'you want me to tell you about it?'

He hesitated. 'All right, but make it quick. We're sailing in half an hour.'

I told him about Sally and John, about John's discovery, the computer, and how I'd come to be found with Sally's body.

'Chris–' he held my eyes – 'are you *sure* you didn't – no, listen, could you have had some sort of blackout, not been truly responsible, you know...'

'I've been over it a hundred times,' I said, mustering all the conviction I could, 'and I know I didn't do it.'

'Then who did?'

I told him about Dave. 'I'm sure it's to do with John's work on AIDS. Dave must be some sort of hit man. I think he's killed John as well.'

'How is any of this going to help you prove

your … your innocence?'

'I need to get to that computer. You see–' I looked up – 'I know what the password is now.'

'How does that help?'

'I'll prove that John's work exists – the police don't even believe that at the moment. It shows why Sally and I were in his flat, and it's the motive for whoever did kill her.'

'A bit thin, isn't it?'

'A cure for AIDS? You could name your own price for that at the moment.'

'Possibly,' he conceded. 'What are you going to do when you get to Watchport?'

I told him and he gazed thoughtfully at me for a long moment.

Then he said, 'Well, as it happens, you're in luck. We're stopping at Watchport to pick up a cargo.'

I tried to thank him but he cut me short. 'I've got work to do. You'd better stay in my cabin for now.'

'What about the crew? I mean, do they know–'

'Not much. The police came to me yesterday about you. I – I promised to tell them if I saw you–'

'And will you?'

He slowly shook his head. 'I'll get the crew

running round now. I'll make up something if necessary and say you left the ship.'

He put his head outside the bridge door, then beckoned me to follow. A seagull wailed overhead. We went down the steps, then immediately into a corridor which led to his cabin.

'Just stay here,' he said when I was inside. 'Lock the door and only open it for me. I'll knock like this.' He showed me. 'I've got to go now. I'll be back when we're at sea.'

I locked the door as he said, then sat on the bed. The silence was gradually filled with background noises, the hum of a generator, sporadic clanging, the rattle of a donkey engine.

I looked around the cabin. It was small, about fifteen feet by ten. Neat and tidy, everything in place. A photo of Alison and their two children … and another of Jill.

I picked it up. She was smiling, the same smile she'd given me in the dream.

There was a jug of water by the bed. I seized and drained it.

Metallic footsteps overhead, someone shouting. I looked cautiously out of the porthole, but it was facing seawards.

I felt dizzy and leaned back against the side of the cabin and closed my eyes. More shouts and a growling noise as something was dragged across the deck.

Perhaps ten minutes later a vibration was transmitted through the cabin-side to my head. The sky moved. I looked out of the porthole again, and very slowly at first, the derricks on the other side of the docks slid by. We passed another ship being loaded, then through a lock and into the estuary. The vibration increased and the ship took on a rocking motion as we reached the sea.

I was still staring out of the porthole at the myriad reflections from the waves when Alan knocked.

I opened the door, he slipped in and locked it behind him.

'We'll be off Watchport in about six hours,' he said. 'Then we have to wait at anchor for another four before going in.'

'Why?'

'There won't be enough water until the tide comes in. When did you last eat?'

'Yesterday morning.'

'I'll see what I can do.'

He went out and was back five minutes later with half a loaf of bread, some butter and cheese, and a mug of coffee.

'All I could get without someone noticing,' he said. And then after a few minutes,

'God, you needed that! I'll get you some more when the crew eat.' He pulled a chair towards me. 'Now, tell me again what you intend doing after we get to Watchport.'

We talked for nearly an hour, then he left me for a while. I watched the sea and the gulls that flew alongside the ship. I could have watched them forever, become one with them. The ultimate in freedom.

The next time Alan came, he had a paper discarded by one of the crew as well as some more food. A blurred likeness of me peered from page two with a description of how I'd escaped. I was described as potentially dangerous and was thought to be in the Bristol area.

That didn't matter. What did matter was that seeing me in print, so to speak, seemed to have given Alan second thoughts. He questioned me closely again about what had happened.

At last, in despair, I seized Jill's picture from the shelf.

'I swear on this, on Jill's memory, that I'm telling you the truth,' I said, meeting his eyes.

He nodded slowly. 'All right, I'll trust you. But if it turns out you've been lying,' he said, with each word distinct, 'I swear I'll break your neck.'

The worst part was waiting at anchor for the tide. I could see the town through the porthole, clustered around the harbour; steam rose from a train in the station beside it and white blobs of houses stretched away up the hill to the church tower silhouetted against the sky. For a moment, I was so homesick I wanted to jump off and swim.

Then at last the pilot's launch appeared from the harbour mouth, ploughing through the choppy sea towards us.

Half an hour later the ship was bumping against the wharf, and a little while after that Alan re-appeared.

'I've sent the crew into town,' he said. 'Let's try and get those cuffs off.'

He led me deep into the ship, through the engine-room to a tiny workshop.

'This is where you're going to have trust me,' he said, grinning for the first time that day. He switched on an electric carborundum wheel and, bracing himself against the bench, held and pushed the cuff against it. Sparks flew, as though from a firework. I closed my eyes.

It was like having a tooth drilled, the noise and the vibrations seemed to go on forever.

Then there was a sharp pain and the noise stopped.

I opened my eyes to see a few drops of blood beading my wrist.

'Sorry about that.' Alan grinned again.

'Worthwhile exchange.' I twisted off the cuff. 'Would you get rid of them for me?'

'I'll drop them overboard tomorrow.'

'Is it dark yet? I'd better get over to Joe's.'

'No, let me scout around first, in case the police are there.'

When he returned twenty minutes later he had Joe with him.

'Chrees!' he embraced me. 'I see you in the papers, the police they ask questions, but I cannot believe.' He really does talk like that. 'I think I never see you again.'

He'd brought his barber's impedimenta with him, and began to set it up.

'See any police?' I asked Alan.

'They've got your place staked out all right,' he said grimly, 'and they've warned all your neighbours to watch out for you–'

'I tell them nosink,' said Joe.

'Did they see you leave?'

'We slipped out through the back yard,' said Alan. 'Nobody saw us.'

Joe had spread a sheet on the floor, now he sat me in a chair in front of a washbasin and began work, first taking off my beard and moustache with clippers, then starting on my hair.

When he gave me the mirror half an hour later, I really couldn't believe it. The face that looked back was clean-shaven and topped with very short, fair hair. He'd even dyed my eyebrows.

'Remember,' he warned me, 'one week and the dark hairs will begin to show.'

'You'd better remember to shave every morning as well,' said Alan. 'Fair hair doesn't go very well with black stubble.'

An hour later, after a shower, a change of clothes and some more food, I felt, as well as looked, a different person. Joe lent me his son's car, an old Vauxhall Viva, and Alan lent me his binoculars, forty pounds and his cash dispenser card. I looked at the latter in astonishment.

'You'll need more than forty quid,' he said gruffly. 'You'd better buy some more clothes, mine look a bit loose on you.'

'Alan, if I'm caught and they find this, you'll be implicated.'

'True. Use it tonight and again tomorrow morning, then post it back to me.'

I left Watchport by a side road and drove slowly to Bridgwater, getting used to the car, then across country to Swindon in case the police had set up roadblocks on the motorway. I stayed in a small anonymous hotel and was up at seven the next morning and on my way back to Oxford.

CHAPTER 13

The Dreaming Spires pricked the skyline as I came down from the Swindon road; the city beneath like a bed upon which Sally and John now slept forever, a bed to which I had to return...

It was just after 8.0. I drove straight to the hospital and found a vantage-point about a hundred yards from the lab entrance, from where with the binoculars I could see without being seen.

My plan was simple as far as it went: to follow Dave and find out where he was staying, then break into the laboratory and get a printout of John's data. I hadn't really thought beyond that. I suppose I intended somehow to force a confession out of Dave and use it with the printout.

The ancillaries arrived at 8.30. Next came Mary at a quarter to nine, then Ron at ten to and Phil just after. Most of the rest streamed in after that. It was so strange watching them climb the steps to the door as though nothing had happened.

Ian arrived at ten past as usual, slamming his car door and running breathlessly across the car park. Dave didn't come until twenty past.

He was in no hurry. He locked the door of his car, an immaculate Mini Cooper, and sauntered over to the lab, one hand in his pocket. I couldn't tear my eyes from him, although the sight of him tightened a band round my chest so that I couldn't breathe.

He was about to go in when another car pulled up by the door. Charles was back, his tan a shade or two deeper. Dave waited for him and they stood outside talking for a moment or two.

I could see every detail of Dave's face, his every hair – suddenly he raised his head and for a moment it was as though he were looking into my eyes. I wanted to duck out of sight, even though I knew it was only an illusion caused by the binoculars.

He turned away and they went inside.

A couple of minutes later, Carey arrived. He climbed out of his Range-Rover, retrieved his briefcase and slammed the door. I heard the solid clunk half a second later. He strode to the steps, his lips pursed in a self-satisfied little smile.

I found myself trembling. What right had

he, had any of them to be free, to just carry on as normal while I had to creep about in disguise?

I waited in the car until I became calmer, then drove to the city centre and bought some clothes (cord jeans, a sweater and sweatshirt), also a razor, soap and toothbrush and a newspaper. I drew another fifty pounds with the cash card and posted it back to Alan as promised, then found a room in an inconspicuous guesthouse called The Pines.

I had some food and coffee and read the paper. My escape only rated a couple of paragraphs now, although the police were still confident of apprehending me at any moment.

Midday found me back at my vantage-point, watching some of the staff drift over to the canteen. Then Dave came out, by himself, and walked over to his car.

It was what I'd been waiting for. I let him drive to the gate, then cautiously followed. He turned right. So did I. There were two cars between us. St Giles ... left into Broad Street ... then right, through the Science Area. So long as there was a car between us, I kept fairly close, hanging back if it stopped or turned off.

Three cars as we waited at the Longwall traffic lights. Then over Magdalen Bridge, the Plains, Cowley Road ... he must be going to John's flat!

Then he jumped an amber light, the car in front of me stopped and by the time we were moving again, he'd completely disappeared. There was nothing I could do but drive on to the flat.

His car wasn't there, so I parked nearby and waited. The house looked so ordinary in the sunshine, so like anywhere else.

As I sat there, thinking about Dave returning to the scene of the crime, it suddenly occurred to me that I was doing just that myself. I was behaving as though I were invisible.

What if the police were watching me now? I cautiously looked round. A front door slammed and a man came out of one of the houses. A curtain above twitched.

My heart hammering, I started the engine and drove slowly away.

Mirror. No police cars, just a taxi. As I drew further away, I began to breathe again.

I drove to the hospital, but there was no sign of Dave or his car, so I went back to the guest-house.

Nor was he there at five, when the laboratory staff went home. It was depressing, but I'd have to try again tomorrow, after I'd got the printout from the computer.

It was nearly dark when I set out for the last time. The air was warm, the city ponderous, almost sleepy. The black silhouettes of the ancient buildings hung in the sky against the sunset while lovers walked below, beneath the trees, their intimacy accentuated by the shadows. The churning in my stomach grew.

The hospital gates. I left the car in the main park and walked over to the laboratory. A nurse passed quickly the other way, clutching a file to her breast. A blackbird briefly coloured the dusk.

I climbed the steps, looked around, then put my hand into the letter-box for the key.

The door opened easily. I shut it gently and waited a few moments in the silence while my eyes adjusted. Then, softly up the stairs.

The main corridor was lit faintly from the lights outside. A 'fridge hummed. An electric clock ticked the half-minute. I slid through the shadows to John's room.

To switch on the light or not? No, tempting fate. I could just make out the screen of the computer.

197

I reached behind it for the switch and the blue glow faintly lit the room. I sat in front of it and began.

John's code, then through the menu; John's code again, reversed... 'Do you want to print?' No. Through his first project, then:

'Password?'

A second's hesitation, then I tapped in DEERCRAP.

'OK,' said the screen. 'Do you want to print?' Yes. A heading: 'Effect of substance P7 on *in vitro* growth of HIV in OKT4 cells.'

Screen after screen filled with densely packed data, tables and formulæ, the printer buzzed like a demented insect while I watched the paper stream from it in waves.

Then it was finished. I'd made no attempt to understand it, that could wait. I tore off the paper, folded it and–

'Thanks, I've been waiting for that.'

My nerves fused and for an instant I was paralysed, then I whipped round. He was about two yards behind me, smiling in the blue light. I didn't think, just went for him. He dodged, tripping me with a foot so that I sprawled on to the floor.

As he stepped past me towards the computer, I grabbed an ankle and heaved.

He staggered and fell against a chair, giving me time to get up. He was at me in a flash, fist lancing for my belly, but I was ready for him, blocked it with my left and lashed out with my right.

He saw it coming and feinted, but it caught the side of his head and he fell back against the computer. The glow was extinguished as it crashed on to the floor.

I kicked, felt my toe catch his leg, then smashed at where I thought his head was. It connected and he went down.

I fell on him, reaching for his neck. He tried to wriggle away but I held on to his jacket. A fist caught the side of my face but I hardly felt it.

We slithered round together on the floor, knocking into chairs and bench-legs while he rained blows at me and I fumbled for his throat. I kept my head down and his fists glanced harmlessly from my scalp. Our breath came in sobs.

Then I found it, his throat, clutched, squeezed, felt my fingers sink in. I was killing him for what he'd done to Sally. I was executing him.

He went limp. My fingers loosened fractionally as I got on top of him for better purchase, then his knee came from nowhere into my crotch.

For a microsecond I felt nothing, just the thump; then the pain roared up through my belly, my chest, my skull. I tried to scream but the pain choked me. I remember rolling off him, clutching at myself, trying to scream, breath escaping in tiny whimpers.

Time didn't exist, just a world of pain stretching into infinity.

I didn't hear him get up, the first thing I was aware of outside myself was a rasping cough.

Then he kicked me. 'I said, have you had enough?' He started coughing again.

I think I said yes, although all I was aware of was the slightest diminishing of the agony, and with it, an overwhelming sense of relief.

He stumbled over to the door and switched on the light, then found a chair and collapsed into it, his chest heaving. I just lay where I was, trying to will the pain away.

After a while, it might have been five minutes, he pulled himself up.

'Well, I suppose I'd better get you down to the nick,' he said.

I looked up at him, and despite everything, found myself laughing at the supreme irony of it.

'What's so damn funny?' he demanded.

'Well, you've got to admit it's good. You handing me over to the police for what you've done...' I laughed some more, although it hurt.

'They're right – you are mad,' he murmured.

'*Mad?* Oh, that's the end. You murder Sally, John too, get me blamed for it and then tell me *I'm* mad.'

He knelt beside me. 'You killed Sally Wytham. I don't know about Devlin, but everyone knows you killed Sally–'

'That's really good. Just keep saying it like that and everyone'll believe you. No problem.'

'And you just tried to kill me,' he said softly.

'I'd try again, if I could. You deserve to die. She didn't.'

'You'd kill me because you think I killed her?'

'I know you killed her. You murdered her.'

'How? How do you know that?'

I hesitated. 'Who else could it be?'

He took another deep breath, then he said, 'I thought it was odd.' A pause. 'Well, if you didn't kill her, and I didn't, then who did?'

He said it so matter-of-factly that I knew it had to be true.

I dragged myself up. 'Who are you?'

'My name's Jones. I'm a DHSS invest-igator.' He took a plastic-covered identifi-cation card from his wallet and handed it to me. 'I was sent here to watch John Devlin, who's suspected of stealing industrial secrets from Parc-Reed Pharmaceuticals.'

CHAPTER 14

I stared at the card for a long moment while my mind tried to take it all in. At last I said:

'Where is he?'

'Devlin? I don't know. I thought you did.'

'He's dead,' I said dully. 'Whoever killed Sally–'

'What makes you say that?'

I shrugged, then winced. 'I'd have heard from him by now.'

'What were you going to do with that?' He indicated the printout.

'Give it to my solicitor, I suppose.'

'Why?'

'It proves some of what I told the police. They didn't believe there was any secret work on AIDS.'

'He'd have shopped you. They all believe you're insane. There's too much evidence against you.'

'What do you believe?'

'That you're in the shit. Do you want to help me?'

'Have I any choice?'

203

'Not really, unless you like prison. How are you feeling?'

'Pretty bloody awful.'

'It'll pass. We'd better be thinking about going.'

'What about this mess?' I indicated the room. 'Hadn't we better clear it up?'

He looked around. 'No,' he said slowly. 'I want the staff, all of them, to know there's been a break-in. In fact, I want them to know what we've got, or at least have some idea.'

'Why?'

'A trap. In fact, I'm going to make it more obvious.' He picked up the printout and stared at it for a moment. 'We'll leave some of this behind, perhaps just the first sheet with the title. I'll get it off one of the other terminals.' He looked up. 'What is the password?'

It meant nothing to him. He went out and a moment or so later, I heard the printer buzzing in the virology lab. Then he was back with the first sheet, which he left on top of the printer.

'Time we were going. You'd better stay at my hotel. We'll pick up your stuff from The Pines tomorrow.'

'How did you know where I was staying?'

'Followed you today. After you'd followed me. Come on.'

He propped open the door with one of the fallen chairs, took a last look round, then switched off the light.

I limped down the stairs after him. He opened the door cautiously, only leaving when he was sure we were unobserved.

'What about my car?' I asked, as we reached his.

'We'll pick it up tomorrow.' He let me in, then drove quickly to where he was staying at the Churchill Hotel. As soon as we were inside his room, a double, he took a large first-aid box from his case.

'Does it still hurt?'

'Yes,' I said feelingly.

'Take a couple of these.' He handed me two unmarked capsules which I swallowed with some water.

Then, to my surprise, he started to examine his face minutely in the mirror and carefully dress the cuts and abrasions with lotion and a styptic pencil.

'No, I'm not being a wimp,' he said, catching my eye. 'If I don't get this bruising down, some clever sod in the laboratory might start thinking.'

He went on working. I glanced at my

watch. To my astonishment, it was only a little after ten.

As he rubbed some of the lotion into his neck, he said, 'You'll have to stay here tonight, but tomorrow I think we'd better make a strategic withdrawal to the Smoke, just in case the police start adding three and four and decide to make a search. Now–' he put the lotion away, pulled open a drawer and took out a bottle of whisky – 'we don't have much time if we're to set this trap up by the morning, so we'd better compare notes.' He splashed whisky into a couple of toothglasses and handed me one.

'Will this be all right on top of those capsules?' I asked.

'As long as you don't have too much. How are you feeling now?'

'A bit better,' I said, surprised. 'What's in–'

'Good. As I said, we don't have much time, so you'd better tell me what you know.'

I told him briefly how I'd come to know John and Sally, and everything I could remember since arriving in Oxford nearly three weeks before.

'So you had no contact with Devlin at all while you were here?' he interrupted.

'None. Haven't the police tried tracing him?'

'I'll tell you about that later. Go on with your story.'

I still found it very difficult to think about what happened that Sunday after Sally's 'phone call, so I skated quickly around it.

'So you've no idea who hit you?' Jones asked.

'I thought it was you.'

He leaned forward. 'Who do you think it was now?'

I felt my mind close over. 'Sorry, I don't know.'

He was silent for a moment. I began asking him about John again, but he cut me short.

'You'll have to bear with me for a little while.' He leaned forward again. 'Listen. I'm going to make some assumptions; you tell me if they're wrong, and why. First, we know that Sally found the password and was then killed. We assume that whoever killed her was also looking for the password, but didn't get it, because if they had they would have wiped the data off the computer.'

I gave a single nod.

He continued. 'I think we can assume that it's someone in the laboratory–'

'But *who*?'

'We'll speculate on that later, but for the

moment we can assume that they're feeling pretty secure now.'

'What about the fact that I've escaped?'

'That'll make them feel even safer if anything, since it looks like an admission of guilt. And lastly–' he bared his teeth briefly – 'we'll assume they still want the data, which is why it's the bait for our trap.

'Now, when that mess we left tonight is found tomorrow, the police'll be called in. They'll show the piece of printout we left to all the staff, so that our man will know that *someone's* got the data, *but he won't know who.* We've somehow got to let him know that it's for sale, and where to apply. How do we do that?'

There was a silence while I grappled with his reasoning, then the ghost of something formed in my mind.

'I've got an idea, but I can't put any shape to it until you tell me how far the police got in tracing John.'

He made a slight gesture of impatience. 'They found his mother in Glasgow, who told them she hadn't seen him for a month, although he had 'phoned her a fortnight before to say that he might be away for a while.'

'America,' I said. 'You must have seen that

letter from NAP.'

'I wondered when you'd remember that.' He took a sip of his drink. 'It all fits. I was in the laboratory for two weeks before you came. Devlin had realized who I was and the Friday before you arrived, he accused me and we had a hell of a row. Then he disappeared and after that, you, his great and probably only buddy, turned up, so I naturally assumed you knew where he was and what he was doing.'

'Have you tried tracing him to America?'

'The police have questioned NAP, who admit to having been in contact with him, but deny sending him to the States. But then again, they would, wouldn't they?'

'But if he'd gone to America,' I said, 'wouldn't he have wiped his data from the computer first? And I still think he would have let me know where he was.'

'Why? Oh, all right, I take your point, he's either in the States or he's dead. Now what was your idea?'

'We send a postcard, apparently from John, to all the lab staff. It would contain a reference to his work and a 'phone number.'

'They'd all try it.'

'All right – how about this? We make a reference to a newspaper on the card and

209

then put the number in the personal column of the paper.'

'Not bad, though we'd have to make the reference pretty obscure – no, it won't work. The police still want to see Devlin since the killing took place in his flat, so they'd be shown the card. They'd be on to us in a second.'

'I hadn't thought of that.'

'I think you're on the right track.' He swallowed the last of his drink and abstractedly poured himself some more. He said slowly, 'We could always leave the message on the computer.'

'But how–?'

'Listen! Our man will have got as far with the program as we did before you realized what the final password was. I think it'll shake him that someone else has got there, but as soon as he's got a minute alone, he won't be able to resist trying the computer again, to see if he can work it out himself. That's when he finds our message.'

'Won't he realize it's a trap?'

'Depends on how we put it.' His eyes moved as he thought. 'I quite like your newspaper idea ... yes ... the message will be a reference to a newspaper, and we'll put a 'phone number in the personal column...'

He turned back to me. 'Is there time to get an advert in the local daily – what's it called?'

'*Oxford Mail.*'

'That's it – can we get it in for Monday?'

'I think so, yes.'

'Better be sure. I wonder if they'd know in reception.'

He tried them and they did – there was time if we placed it in the morning.

I said, 'How do you know the police won't work this one out?'

He thought quickly. 'Because I'll be there to make sure they don't. They're bound to ask me–'

'Don't the police know who you are?'

'Only a couple of the higher-ups. As I was saying, they're bound to ask the visiting computer expert about this mysterious program, so I'll fiddle around with it a bit, then say I can't understand it. Our man will heave a sigh of relief at that–' He stopped short. 'And maybe I'll be able to spot him then. We'll see,' he finished abruptly.

I said, 'How are you going to word the message?'

'Just "Mail on Monday" should do it. After "Continue for Project II".' He reached for his jacket. 'I'll go on my own, there's no point in you taking any more risks than you have to. Why don't you try making some sense of that while you're waiting?' He pointed to the printout and then was gone.

I did as he suggested because I needed something to distract me. As I went through it, some of the phrases brought back John very clearly, especially the night he'd shown me the AIDS virus on the electron microscope. Was he in America now, trying to sell his discovery? I couldn't make up my mind. Part of me was still sure he was dead.

Jones was back after forty minutes.

'You've done it?' I asked.

'Piece of cake.' He poured us both some more whisky and lit a cheroot. 'Well, what do you think of it?' He indicated John's data.

'I've only had time to glance through, but it strikes me as a brilliant piece of work. I have a feeling that it's not quite finished,' I added.

'But finished enough to hawk around?'

'Yes.'

There was a short silence while he sipped his drink, then he said, 'So Devlin had you believing it was his own work?'

'I still think so. This work is his style…'

Jones shook his head. 'No, he pinched it

from Parc-Reed. My brief was to find out what he was doing with it.'

'If it really *is* Parc-Reed's discovery, why are they so worried?' I asked. 'Surely with their facilities, they could have the work finished before John did.'

'They think that what he's doing is trying to alter it just enough to escape their patent, so that he can sell it abroad.'

I picked up the printout. 'This doesn't read like that, it reads like original work.'

'I didn't say Devlin isn't clever.'

'What if you've got it the wrong way round?' I was emboldened by the whisky. 'What if Parc-Reed are trying to steal it from John?'

'No, it wasn't his idea, originally–'

'How do you know that?'

'And even if it was,' he continued as though I hadn't spoken, 'he was under contract at the time, so it still belongs to Parc-Reed.'

'But they sacked him, so they'd broken the contract.'

He shook his head. 'Doesn't work like that. Anyway, we'll soon know now that I've got his data.'

I sat very still. 'Are you saying that your job's finished?'

'In a manner of speaking. But I want to

know where Devlin is, or whether, as you think, he's dead, and the only way I can see of doing that at the moment, is to find out who killed Sally.'

I relaxed again. 'D'you mind if I ask you a couple of questions?'

He glanced at his watch. 'All right, so long as you remember that I've got to be up bright and early tomorrow.'

I hesitated. 'You do believe that it wasn't me?'

'You wouldn't be here if I didn't.'

'What made you believe me?'

He smiled wryly. 'I've found that when someone's *in extremis*, like you were tonight, they're nearly always telling the truth.'

'I'm glad for that. How did you know I'd be there?'

He grinned. 'I spotted your binoculars flashing in the sun this morning, so I let myself out at the back, circled round and watched you.'

'How did you know it was me?'

'I didn't at first, that disguise is good. But logically it had to be you, and once I'd realized that, I could see it was. So I allowed you to follow me at lunch-time to make sure, then ditched my car, found a taxi and picked you up at Devlin's flat. Then followed you back to the hospital, then to The Pines. I was sure you'd want to get at the computer, so I waited for you there.' He felt his neck gingerly. 'I wasn't expecting quite so much resistance.'

'And I wasn't expecting your knee...'

'No, that's the beauty of it. Has the pain gone now?'

'Not quite.'

He took some of the capsules from his box and handed them to me. 'Take a couple more now, and if it still hurts in the morning, another two.' As I swallowed them, he said, 'I'd better do my face again, then I think it's time for bed.'

Although I was so tired, I lay awake for a long time. My mind wandered drowsily over the day's events as I listened to the steady breathing of the man whom, a short while ago, I had tried to kill.

CHAPTER 15

We'd made love, Sally and I, and I slept, except that another part of me was watching, knowing what was about to happen.

The telephone rang… 'Answer it for God's sake,' I mumbled, then jerked up with a shout of terror. Then I saw where I was and collapsed with relief.

Still the telephone rang. I reached for it.

'Hel–' Pips, then a coin was dropped. 'Hello?'

'That you, Chris? It's Tom Jones here – sorry if I woke you, but I'm about to put the advert in the paper and wanted to check the number… Are you there?'

'Yes.'

'Well, we're in luck. I found out this morning that if you put a prefix in front of the extension you can ring straight through to the hotel room without going through the switchboard, d'you follow me? Anyway, I thought I'd better try it first. How are you feeling?'

'Not sure yet.' I looked at the clock by his

bed. It was just after eleven. 'What happened this morning?'

He chuckled. 'It went well, but I think we'd better head for the Smoke first thing this afternoon. I'll come back lunch-time and tell you about it then.' He disconnected.

I crawled out of bed and took stock of my body. I had a headache, felt dizzy and my groin ached. I took the last two capsules with some milk I found in the 'fridge and then ran a deep, hot bath.

I felt a bit better after that, but still just lay on the bed waiting for the pain to go.

Jones walked in at a quarter past twelve. 'Hello. Hungry?'

'I am a bit.'

'Wrap yourself round these.' He handed me a pack of sandwiches and an individual apple pie.

'Thanks. So what happened this morning? You seem very cheerful.'

'I am. It went like a dream.' He sat down on the bed and told me as I ate.

He hadn't wanted to get there too early in case it looked suspicious, but had managed to arrive at the same time as Ron.

'Which was just as well. The ancillaries had found the mess we left but hadn't done anything about it. Ron 'phoned the police straight away, but he'd have still had plenty of time to remove our calling card if he'd wanted. He didn't get the chance, 'cos I stuck to him like gin and it.'

Then the police had arrived and, as Jones had guessed, they'd interviewed everyone and shown them the piece of printout. Then he'd been asked to find the program from which it came, but had regretfully confessed himself baffled.

'You watched them all for reaction?' I asked.

'Like a hawk, but I didn't spot anything. Not a flicker.'

'So what do we do now?'

'Leave our brew to ferment over the weekend and wait for someone to contact us on Monday.'

'What did you put in the advert in the end?'

'Oh yes. I put "JSD 123 – for data, ring 732891 at eight sharp tonight."'

'And that definitely comes out on Monday?'

He nodded.

'What do we tell him?' I asked. 'I mean, he'll want to know who we are.'

'We just tell him that if he wants the goods, it'll cost him ten thousand. We've got to convince him we're only concerned with selling.'

'Then what?'

'The really interesting bit, we arrange a meeting. We'll have to play that by ear. And now,' he said, overriding my next question, 'I think it's time we were on our way to London.'

'What about my car?' I asked.

'We'd better not leave it at the hospital,' he said thoughtfully. 'Give me the keys and I'll walk over and get it now. We can leave it here for the weekend.'

'Just one other thing,' I said as I handed them over. 'Did anyone connect the break-in with me, with my escape?'

'As a matter of fact, they did. There was quite a little discussion about it in the rest-room.'

'Who started it?'

'Well, that was rather odd. It was your little monkey-faced pal, Ian Lambourne.'

As I waited for him to return, I pondered on the significance of this, but couldn't see it.

Half an hour later, having called at the guest-house to collect my things and settle the bill, we were on the M40 to London. Jones was still in a high good humour, so I tried pumping him about his job, and to my surprise, he gave me some of his life-story.

He'd run away from home at the age of sixteen to join the Army and after a few years had joined the police. He'd become a detective in the Fraud Squad and also an expert on computers before leaving the Force for reasons he wouldn't go into. After a period of temporary jobs and the dole, he'd found his present work of investigating fraud and corruption in the NHS.

'You'd be amazed at how much there is,' he said. 'I didn't believe my guv'nor at first when he told me the DHSS loses more than £100 million a year through villainy, but I believe it now.'

'Something to do with low pay, perhaps,' I suggested.

'Not always, no. Some people want more however much they already have.'

I asked how he'd come to get this particular assignment since it involved a commercial company, and after some hesitation, he told me how a complaint from Parc-Reed had ended up on his boss's desk and that he (Jones) had asked to work on it when he heard it involved a cure for AIDS. His brother was a hæmophiliac who had the disease.

I was watching his profile against the window as he spoke.

'He's on AZT at the moment, or Zidovu-dine as you're supposed to call it now.' His expression belied the lightness of his words. 'It's doing him some good, I suppose, but it does have some nasty side-effects.'

'How long has he had AIDS?' I asked.

'Two – two-and-half years.'

'He's not doing badly, then. If he can hang on a bit longer, maybe he's got a chance.'

He smiled mirthlessly. 'That's what they all say: "If he can hang on a bit longer, Mr Jones, then he might just be in a position to hang on a bit longer."' He sighed. 'Sorry. It's better sometimes than others. You see, AZT's given him hope. Hope's important. I think he is feeling better, but another, new drug might make all the difference. That's why I wanted to have a go at Devlin when I heard about him.' The muscles in his face clenched. 'People who try to make a fast buck out of AIDS, they ... they're as bad as drug-pushers, they deserve all they've got coming to them.'

Suddenly, he was Dave again, the man who terrorized, who went for the balls – but I could understand why, now.

I tried to tell him about the John I'd

known, who'd struggled up from nowhere, whose experience had conditioned him to be always an outsider.

'We've all had problems,' said Jones unsympathetically. 'You should know that.'

I told him about the evidence I'd seen of John's scientific brilliance, genius almost, and how I was convinced that P7 was his own work.

'Even if that were true,' he said, 'if Devlin made the discovery while he was employed by Parc-Reed, and on their premises, then the law is in their favour.'

'D'you know that for a fact?'

There was a silence. Then:

'If you mean, have I seen it in writing, then the answer's No. But I've been assured that it's the case.'

'By whom?'

'By my department.'

'Who in turn, perhaps, have been assured by Parc-Reed.'

For a moment he looked annoyed, then his face relaxed into a grin. 'All right, you've made your point. I'll check it out, just to satisfy you.'

By now we were well into London and couldn't be far from the hotel, which didn't leave me much time.

'Who do you think did it?' I asked abruptly.

'I don't know.'

'You must have some idea.'

He pulled up at some traffic lights. 'My last job showed me that you have to suspect literally everybody. Also, that speculation tends to leave you peering up your own backside– Ah, the hotel's just round here.'

He parked outside and came in with me to check the reservation.

'Sure you've got everything you need?' he asked.

My pent-up thoughts threatened to burst as the loneliness of the weekend stretched in front of me.

'I'll pick you up Sunday evening. Shall we say nine? I'll have arranged a room for you at the Churchill by then.'

'Don't go yet. Have a coffee with me,' I said. 'Please.'

He hesitated. 'All right.'

I could tell that he didn't want to. I said, 'There's so much going round my head, I – I've just got to talk about it. Speculate.'

He smiled then. 'All right,' he said again. 'But let's make it a beer.'

As we waited at the bar he said awkwardly, 'I'm sorry about leaving you here, but my flat's very small, and I haven't seen my girlfriend for a week...'

'It's OK, I understand–'

'So take as long as you need to get your speculating off your chest.'

We took our beer to a corner table.

'Before you begin,' he said, 'remember that the basic requirements of Motive and Opportunity still apply, it's just that their parameters are wider. Now, first, who are the people we're looking at?'

'Ron, Phil and Carey,' I said without hesitation. 'They're the obvious ones.'

'What about Charles and Ian?'

'That's ridiculous, Charles was abroad at the time, so he didn't have the opportunity, and Ian–'

'How do you know that?'

'Well, because...'

'You pulled me up just now over the law being in Parc-Reed's favour, now you're making the same mistake.'

'*Touché*. All right, but what about Ian, what motive could he have?'

'Money. He's only a basic grade Scientific Officer, so with two kids he'd be critically hard up. And, he's in a perfect position to know exactly what Devlin's been doing. So you see what I mean, having to suspect everybody?'

'All right, you've made your point.'

We both smiled.

'Good. So let's consider the three you mentioned, starting with Ron.'

'Well, he had the opportunity and he couldn't bear John, to start with.'

'Go on.'

I told him how Ron had tried to get rid of me from the moment I'd arrived, how he played down John's disappearance and how he'd finally set the police on to me.

'How d'you know he did that?'

'Sally and I worked it out. It happened just after Ron really piled the pressure on, and he's a Mason with police connections. Who else could it have been?'

'As a matter of fact, it was me.' I stared at him. 'Ron wasn't the only one who wanted to get rid of you. At the time, I thought it might flush Devlin out – I realize now I was wrong.'

I slumped back in my seat. 'D'you know, I couldn't understand at the time why Ron was so much easier with me the next day.'

Jones leaned forward. 'But that would have been when he announced that he'd had that 'phone call from Devlin. *Was* it Devlin, or someone else saying they were Devlin?'

I said slowly, 'We've only got Ron's word

225

for it that there was a 'phone call.'

'You're learning.'

'But it all just leaves us where we started. I can't think of another motive for him, other than that he couldn't stand John.'

'But we certainly can't eliminate him, can we? Let's go on to Phil.'

I sat up and thought. 'Well, Phil may have been jealous of John, but he wouldn't have killed Sally. He loved her.'

'But it was unrequited love, the worst kind. First Devlin got in his way, then you. Don't forget, I saw his statement to the police, he did more than any of them to put the rope around your neck.'

'I can believe that,' I said quietly. 'But where does John's data fit into it?'

'Perhaps it doesn't, in which case we're up shit creek, because he won't go for our bait. So let's think about Carey.'

I thought hard about Carey. 'Motive *and* opportunity,' I said at last. 'He knew about John's data and he wanted it.'

'How do you know that?'

I explained how Carey had quizzed me and how he'd given himself away when he'd claimed he didn't have the results of the work John was doing for him.

'But he might have just wanted to know

226

what was going on in his own laboratory,' said Jones, 'which would be reasonable enough.'

'No, he wanted that data, I'm sure of it. And there's the fact that he sacked John and then took him back, as though he'd found out what he was doing and was waiting for him to finish it.'

Jones finished his beer. 'Even if you're right, there's a big difference between coveting Devlin's work and killing for it.'

'D'you want another?' I asked, pointing at his glass.

'I hadn't better, since I'm driving.' He grinned ruefully. 'I lost my licence a year or so back and once is quite enough. Besides, I promised Holly I wouldn't be too late, so I'd better go soon. But d'you see what I mean now about speculation?'

'I suppose so.'

'Well, no harm's done if it's got it off your chest. Let's wait and see who walks into our trap on Monday. Oh, there's something I didn't tell you.' He came closer. 'I didn't just leave the message on the computer last night, I left a trip-wire as well, so that I can see in the morning whether anyone's been into the program.'

'Will it tell you who it is?'

'No, because they'll have used Devlin's password. But it will tell us that the bait's been taken.'

I searched his face. 'And you do think it's one of those three, don't you?'

'Or Charles or Ian.' He eyes became faraway. 'Or X.'

'Who's X?'

'Just someone we haven't thought of.'

CHAPTER 16

At a quarter to eight on Monday evening, we sat waiting in Jones's room, he next to the telephone on the desk, me on the bed beside the extension.

A handkerchief lay unfolded on the desk, to disguise his voice. 'He'll almost certainly use one too,' he said, 'but listen on the extension – just in case you can catch something that gives him away. But for Christ's sake, don't say anything.'

And so we both waited.

The weekend hadn't been as bad as I feared. Thinking was what I was most afraid of, but the hotel had its own small library, and that and the television held most of my thoughts at mind's length.

Jones came over to see me on Saturday evening for a drink and brought his girl-friend, Holly. I suppose I'd expected a street-wise, self-confident Londoner, but instead found myself talking to an attractive, uncomplicated girl from South Devon. Between them, they eased the evening away.

On the way back to Oxford on Sunday, I asked him about his cover job in the laboratory.

'Oh, it's a *bona fide* job,' he said, 'their system needed modifying and I've modified it. Mind you,' he added with a grin, 'it's just as well things have come to a head now, I couldn't have spun it out for much longer.'

Monday was torture. Jones didn't come back or contact me and I spent the day prowling my room, unable to keep still, but not daring to go out.

He 'phoned me from his room just after six. 'The bait's been taken,' he said softly, 'just one person.' He insisted that we were ready by the telephone at seven, 'just in case he rings early to catch us off balance,' he said.

And so here we were, not saying anything, not looking at each other, just waiting as the adrenalin twisted my innards into knots...

Ten to eight.

Five to. Jones shifted uneasily in his chair. An itch on my back had to be scratched; as I reached for it, the bells jangled discordantly.

Together, we lifted the receivers.

'Yes?' said Jones neutrally into the handkerchief.

'Oh, hello there,' said a cheery voice, 'is this some sort of competition? If so, I'm interested.'

'No, it isn't. Please get off the line.'

He replaced his headpiece and motioned me to do the same.

Another ring.

'Come on, what is it?' The same voice. 'I'm interested, what's going on?'

Jones closed his eyes. He said: 'It's a woman. I'm waiting for a call from a woman. Please don't screw it up for me. All right?' He pressed the button without waiting for an answer.

'Cretin,' he said between his teeth.

'Could it have been him, trying us out?'

'No, not twice.'

We waited. Two minutes past eight. Three. I think we both jumped as it rang.

'Yes?'

'I'm phoning for information regarding JSD.'

I nearly dropped the receiver. It was a metal voice, the voice of a robot, the sort of voice a computer would use.

Jones was urgently signalling me to be quiet.

'We have that information,' he said, his own voice pitched low so that I could hardly

231

recognize it.

'We?'

'Myself and a colleague.'

'Where did you get it?'

'From the computer in the National Microbiology Laboratory.'

'How did you know the password?'

'It's our job to find passwords.'

'Who are you?'

'People who wish to do business.'

'The work is for sale, then?'

'For the right price, yes.'

'Why was the line engaged at eight when I first tried?'

'A time-waster. I got rid of him.'

'What is the right price?'

'Ten thousand. No arguments.'

A pause.

'I would need to examine the computer printout before agreeing to that price.'

'That would be reasonable. I suggest we meet.'

'Very well.'

'I suggest we meet at–'

'No.' The voice cut him off. 'We will meet at a time and place of my choosing. Or there will be no meeting.'

I could see Jones thinking furiously.

'When and where do you suggest?'

'Tonight. Ten o'clock. There is a small industrial site at the end of Bridge Street in Osney Town. Do you know it?'

He looked quickly at me and I nodded. Sally had shown me Osney Town.

'Yes. We'll be there at ten. How will we know you?'

'There will be only one of you.'

'No,' said Jones emphatically. 'I think you will agree on reflection that ... we have more to lose.'

Brilliant!

There was a longer pause. Then:

'Very well. You will know me when I wish you to know me.' The line clicked dead.

Jones gently replaced his receiver and turned to me. 'What do you think?'

'What the hell was that voice?'

'A voice synthesizer. Used by people who've had their larynx removed. You hold it against your throat and whisper, and ... well, you heard the noise it makes.'

'Who would be able to get one of those?'

'Oh, any of the people we suspect. Well, what do you think?'

'I don't know, you're the expert.'

He looked thoughtful. 'It could be a trap. Or a try-out. We don't have a lot of choice. Come on, we'll take your car, he migh recognize mine.'

'Already? It's only–'

'He'll be there an hour early, maybe more. I want to get there first.'

He took down his case, opened a compartment built into the side and took out a small but evil-looking automatic.

'Bloody hell–'

'I was a Boy Scout,' he said as he checked. 'You know: be prepared.' He stuffed it into his pocket.

When we got to the Viva, he held out his hand. 'I'll drive, if you don't mind.'

I didn't really mind, it was just that his peremptory manner could grate sometimes. I handed the keys over.

'Which way?' he said when we were belted in.

Osney Town consists of three parallel streets of artisans' cottages, rather like Jericho, to the west of the city. I don't know why it's called 'town', it's really an island, bounded by the Thames on one side and a backwater on the others. Cars can only gain across via a bridge on one side.

As we crossed it Jones said, 'Where now?'

'raight down here.' I indicated the of the three streets. To our left lay with pleasure boats moored along the bank beside a brightly lit pub. We drove slowly down Bridge Street, past the line of cars parked outside the freshly painted terraces.

Jones glanced at his watch. 'Twenty-five past. I hope we're ahead of him.'

A crossroads. To our left, the river again, lined with trees. About fifty yards ahead were a pair of corrugated iron gates, open. We drove on.

The terraces gave way to a chainlink fence overgrown with weeds.

Through the gates. Sheds on the right with a row of vehicles outside, a truck, a Range-Rover, a Ford Transit with 'Thames Water Authority' painted on the side. The glint of the river lay ahead. Over to the right there was a wharf with three or four barges drawn together beside a crane.

He drove slowly forward to an open tarmac space. Ahead of us was a weir-pool and beyond it, a lock-keeper's hut, unmanned at this time of the evening. A boat floated high in the lock beside it and someone was winding the handle to open the gates.

We stopped for a moment.

'Can't see anyone,' said Jones, looking around. 'Perhaps we've done it.'

He moved forward again, turned right near

the edge of the pool, then reversed behind some bushes until he found a point through which he could see to the gates. He switched off the engine and all we could hear was the roar of the water surging through the hatches from the river behind us into the weir-pool.

'Now we wait,' he said softly.

'Why don't we have a look around?'

'Because if he is already here, he'll be watching us and he'll be well hidden. It would just make it easier for him to pick us off if he wanted. By staying here, in the car, we can watch the gates, we can make a quick getaway if we have to, and if he *is* already here, we force him to make the first move.'

'What if we do see him?'

'Nothing. The most important thing is to identify him; after that, play it by ear.'

We settled back and waited. Jones lit a cheroot. A cat stalked regally past the front of the car. The curtain of noise from the weir was occasionally punctuated with an explosion of quacks from some argumentative ducks. We didn't say much.

As it grew darker the bats awoke and flitted around us. Laughter rang from another late boat as it rose in the lock.

The tension, which had eased in me,

tightened again as ten approached. It was nearly dark, the moon a mere nail-clipping in the sky, but my eyes, accustomed, could see nearly everything. The dark bulk of the sheds. The crane against the sky. The pale form of the Transit. A shimmer on the water.

Ten o'clock.

Nothing. I stuck to my seat.

Five past. A moorhen cried out, disturbed by a couple crossing the footbridge over the weir.

Ten past. Nothing, just the roar of the water. An ache in the small of my back was growing worse and I shifted to ease it.

A quarter past. I said softly, 'D'you think he's coming?'

'Doesn't look like it. We'll give him another fifteen minutes.'

I looked down at my hands as a sense of anti-climax, then defeat, overcame me. Stupid to think he'd walk into so obvious a trap.

At half past, Jones said quietly, 'He's not coming. We'd better get back to the hotel and think about what to do next.' He started the engine. 'Keep a lookout just in case.'

He wound up his window, switched on the lights and edged forward. The beam caught the barges and crane–

A roar, light flooded the car and galloped towards us from the right... Jones tried to accelerate, too late – the light smashed into us, carried us sideways with its momentum to the edge of the pool. As I looked down at the rushing water, the front nearside wheel slipped over the side.

Jones found reverse and frantically gunned the motor, the back wheels screeched as they spun on the tarmac ... the light roared again, pushed, heaved ... we shifted and the other front wheel went over...

I shouted, screamed as the light filled the car, still roaring...

We hung, paralysed, the water below foamed in our lamps, then the concrete edge of the pool scraped at the bottom of the Viva as we toppled over.

CHAPTER 17

The water came at me. I was hurled against the seat-belt as everything went dark green.

I thought the car would turn over, but incredibly, it righted and we surfaced, water dashing against the sides. The walls moved past as we turned like a wheel in the pool.

Water was flooding in through the floor… I shouted as it reached my knees, scrabbled for the door handle–

Then I was jerked round.

'Shut up! Listen to me!' Jones's face, close to mine. His grip tightened. 'Do nothing! Do you understand?'

I nodded.

'Now, undo your seat-belt.'

His eyes on me, I reached down beneath the water, fumbled, found the button and the belt slid free.

'Listen,' he said, still holding me, 'if you try to get out now, we'll be trapped. We must let the car sink. Do you understand?'

Terrified, I nodded. The water crept over my belly.

'Can you swim?'

'Yes, but–'

'We let the car go under, then you open the door slowly, slide through and float up.' The water touched my chest, blotting out the windscreen. 'Find the door catch now … OK? Take a deep breath just before we go under and don't do anything till I push your arm.' The water reached his chin. 'Don't cock it up, because I've got to come out your side too, mine's smashed–'

I breathed in as his voice cut off, my ears filled and the water closed over my head.

A faraway sound of bubbles and swirling. I opened my eyes and the beam of the head-lamps seemed to surround us as we hung suspended in the green water.

My lungs were aching already, why hadn't I breathed deeper, why doesn't Jones–

A deep boom and the car shuddered as we struck something. The hand on my arm gripped and pushed, my fingers closed round the catch and I leaned against the door.

It opened slowly, then stuck. I pushed harder, there was a grinding noise as the car shifted and the door opened a few more inches.

I thrust an arm through the gap and my

fingers touched masonry. We were wedged against the wall of the pool.

I twisted round in my seat so that my back was against the door, then felt up through the gap until my fingers found the ridge at the roof's edge... I pulled ... and by turning my head sideways, squeezed it through, then tried to get my feet on the seat ... but one of them caught in the handbrake ... it wouldn't come loose... I felt Jones pulling it, freeing it, and then I was pushing on the foam of the seat ... the car shifted, trapping my chest, air bubbled from my mouth, then the car shifted again. I went on pushing and my belly, then my pelvis, came through and I was free...

Still holding the roof, I turned in the water, found Jones's head, he didn't seem to be moving... I got my knees on the roof and felt it give as I hauled at his shoulders, then I could see his arms, his body in the green light—

I couldn't wait any longer, kicked against the car, the current took me and the light faded...

I broke surface, breathed and heaved air into my lungs as though I'd never stop, then realized I was still holding Jones's jacket.

I pulled him up. He was quite limp. I

looked round. The current had taken us down to the barges. I reached out and touched a rusty side, felt my way round to the bow.

Steps, leading out of the water. I kicked feebly towards them, dragging Jones with me. The steps were slippery with weed. I scrambled up, keeping hold of him, and once I was on the concrete, twisted round, and hauled him up.

He didn't move. I turned him on his back. His face stared at the sky, white, his mouth hanging open. I pinched his nose and breathed in, held his chin and clamped my mouth over his.

His chest moved, bubbled. Again. And again. Was I doing it properly?

On and on. No sign of life, I should have gone for help, should have–

He twitched. I carried on. Then he coughed, struggled on to his side and retched violently, bringing up a quart of river water.

'Are you all right?'

'Yeah–' A fit of coughing took him, then he lay still for a while, breathing his only movement. Then his head turned to me.

'Thanks,' he said.

It was nearly a mile back to the hotel and we

were both shivering uncontrollably by the time we'd walked back.

I'd already thought about explaining our appearance. We went straight up to reception, ignoring the looks that came our way, and demanded our keys. As the girl handed them to us, I snarled, 'If pushing people off punts is what all your students find funny, God help the rest of the country when they get out...'

I just caught the tail-end of a grin as I turned away.

'Well done,' said Jones when were back in his room.

'Oh, once you understand the mentality of this city, it's easy. Anything, but *anything*, the students do is to be regarded as fun. How are you feeling?'

'Bloody awful. I'm going to have a hot bath before anything else and I suggest you do the same. Got enough spare clothes?'

I nodded.

'See you in a minute, then.'

The bath warmed me but left me torpid and strangely unconcerned about what had happened. All I wanted to do was to go to bed, but since Jones was expecting me, I went reluctantly along to his room.

He was lying propped up against his

pillows, his face flushed, a glass of whisky in his hand. 'Help yourself,' he said, waving his other hand at the bottle.

As I did, he said in disgust, 'A right pair of nurds we are. He had us sussed from the start, didn't he?'

'If you say so.' Just at that moment, I didn't care. The spirit left a warm track deep inside me and I helped myself to more.

'So who was it?' he demanded.

'No idea.'

He reached for pen and paper. 'Well, we'll just have to go through the bloody lot of them again until we work it out.'

I groaned. 'Not now, please. Can't we leave it till tomorrow?'

'No, we can't,' he snapped. 'Now's the time to think about it while it's still fresh in our heads. And the best time to go for him, while he's least expecting it.'

With a sudden movement, he raised himself and sat on the side of the bed. 'Give me some more of that Scotch, it might kill some of the germs I swallowed with the river.'

He poured some, tried it, then picked up his pack of cheroots and extracted one. 'Well, the first thing is, he knew all along it was a trap.' He flung the empty packet viciously against the wall. 'Obviously, he 'phoned us from nearby, then went straight there and waited for us.' He lit the cheroot. 'Did you get a look at what he was driving?'

I shook my head.

'God, I feel sick. We thought we were being so clever, while all the time he was leading us like a pig with a ring in its nose. The question is, does he know who we are?'

I assumed this was rhetorical and didn't answer.

'If he does,' Jones continued, 'will he tell the police? No, I don't think so, he meant it just now, he was trying to kill us. So who the hell is he?'

He seized the pen and paper again, and for a quarter of an hour made me go through the familiar list of names with him. It got us nowhere, although perhaps I wasn't really trying.

He hunted for another cheroot, then remembered he'd just smoked the last.

'I'll go down and get some. Can't think without them.'

When he'd gone, I picked up the list and stared at it.

Ron. Phil. Carey. Charles. Ian.

They were just names, hieroglyphics, they meant nothing. They were not concerned with killing, or traps and countertraps.

Jones came back, cheroot in mouth. 'We've been looking at it from the wrong angle,' he announced. '*You* are what we should be concentrating on.'

'Me?' I said stupidly.

'You've been the closest to our friend and survived, when he belted you after you found Sally. I'll bet there's something locked away in your subconscious that could help–'

'I don't think so.'

'It's worth a try. Let's go through it detail by detail–'

'No.'

'In case there's something–'

'*No!*'

'Listen.' He sat beside me. 'It might do you some good. Talking about it, I mean.'

'Stuff your amateur psychiatry!' I tried to get up but he caught my arm.

'In this instance, the psychiatrists are right.'

'How do you know?' I sneered.

'Because I've been through it myself.'

'Bollocks!'

'It's true.' He regarded me steadily. 'I used to be scared of blood. Fainted when I saw it. Because of my brother.' He drew heavily on his cheroot. 'And the more I pretended there was no problem, the worse it got. But I was forced to come to terms with it, and now I'm … well, better than I was.'

He met my gaze and shrugged, and I believed him.

'So tell me what happened,' he said, almost spoiling it by not waiting for me.

After a long moment, I began. Told him how I'd moved in with her. About Sunday morning. 'I woke up and found her gone.' A monotone. 'Then she 'phoned, said she was at John's flat, that she'd found the password.'

'Did she say what it was?'

'No. I worked it out later. In prison.'

'So how d'you think she found it?'

I shook my head. 'I've no idea.'

'All right, what happened after she 'phoned you?'

'I drove round. Parked outside. The front door wasn't locked so I–'

'Did you see anyone?'

'I – I don't think so.' I swallowed. 'I pushed it open … she was lying there on the bed, I thought she was larking around…'

'Come on,' said Jones urgently. 'You're doing fine. What happened next?'

'Oh yes. There were sheets of Parc-Reed notepaper on the floor, Parc-Reed in big red letters–' My head jerked up– 'That's how she found the password!'

'You see?' said Jones, 'you'd never have worked that out without thinking it through. What did you do then?'

'I – I made some comment about Sleeping Beauty, went to kiss her, that's when I realized… Oh God!'

'Was she fully dressed?'

'Yes.'

'Now think, think about that room. Was there anything that might suggest someone else was there?'

I thought. 'No.'

'All right. Then what?'

'Her face – her eyes were open, staring, her neck was bruised–'

'Did you touch her?'

'I turned her over. Then I just stared at her.'

'For how long?'

'I don't know. I just remember coming to on the floor. I thought – I hoped, it was a dream.'

'Did you hear anything, any noises?'

'No.'

'Did you see anything?'

'No. There were just the bed legs, the carpet, the dust, and–' I jumped.

'What? What is it? You saw something,

didn't you?'

'No,' I lied, 'just the carpet–'

He pulled me round. 'You saw something.'

'No.'

'What was it? Look at me.'

He gripped my shoulders and against my will, I looked up. His eyes were light brown, hazel…

'*What was it?*'

'A pair of shoes.'

'A pair… What shoes?'

I replied tonelessly. 'The same shoes I saw in the disused floor above the lab when I was hiding from you. Wednesday. When I stayed behind to have a go at the computer.'

'Whose–?'

'They were John's shoes,' I said in a dead voice.

He made me go over everything again, then he looked away, absently tapping the table-top with a fingernail.

'Suspect X,' he said at last, as I'd known he would. 'I felt sure he was still around, now I know why.'

'It doesn't mean that–'

'Yes, it does.' He thought some more. 'No wonder the bastard's been out of sight and yet a jump ahead of us all the time. He's been camping out just over our bloody heads. No, listen! He knew I was about to pull the switch on him, but he needed more time – you said yourself that his work seemed unfinished, that's what he's been–'

'But he wouldn't have killed Sally!' I burst out.

'Why not? She was a threat to him. When she found him there, she knew everything … and she hated him, you told me your-self–'

'Not hated–'

'Hell hath no fury…? She'd have told everyone and I'd have been able to stop him, at least that's what he thought, so he killed her. Then set you up to take the rap.'

'But why was he in the flat?'

He closed his eyes a moment. 'The other letters, the ones from North American Pharmaceuticals. He didn't want anyone finding them, didn't realize I'd already seen them–' He turned back to me. 'Were they there when you found Sally?'

'I don't know.'

'Did the police mention them?'

'No.'

'Then he'd got them, and was dreaming about catching his plane to the States, but then you escaped, and the next thing he knows, we've set a trap for him. So he tries to kill us. No wonder he used a voice synthesizer, you'd have recognized him straight away.' He paused. 'I'm sorry about this. You liked him, didn't you?'

'Yes, I liked him.' Snatches of his last letter came back to me. 'I'm nearly there … if they leave me in peace … holding out for the best offer…'

Jones said, 'I think we've got enough now to hand it over to the police, it's–'

'I want to talk to him first.'

'For God's *sake!* He murdered your girl and then set you up for it. You think he's going to listen to you?'

'You listen, there's something you haven't thought of, or maybe you have. The police'll be far more interested in recapturing me than listening to a wild theory from you. And even if you did persuade them to do anything, if he's not there, or you miss him, then I'm back in the–'

'I shan't need to say anything about you.'

'No? So how will you explain your theory? I dreamed it, Officer? They'll realize soon enough that I'm involved–'

'I'm not convinced you're right – but what do you suggest?'

'We get him ourselves.'

'Too risky.'

'I've nothing to lose. And quite a lot to gain.'

He considered me thoughtfully. 'I don't think you want to talk to him at all. More like beat the truth out of him.'

'Something like that.'

He smiled faintly. 'All right. But if we do get him, we're handing him over. I'll see that you're cleared. Agreed?'

I nodded.

He asked me to describe the disused floor and as I did, he emptied, dried and refilled his gun with fresh cartridges.

Then we drove the short distance to the hospital. We didn't speak.

I felt … nothing. No anger, no sorrow, not even a desire to get it over. Perhaps there was nothing left to feel with.

We parked out of sight of the laboratory. Jones said, 'You must do everything I indicate in absolute silence. Keep behind me, and when we get to the room, I go in first, you wait till I call you.'

We walked as close to the walls as we could, so as not to be seen from above. Jones extracted the key and we slipped inside. Waited two minutes. No sound.

He flashed his torch for an instant, then we crept upstairs. Ducked beneath the tapes. When we reached the landing above, we waited again. Another flash. The padlock and hasp hung uselessly, but the door was closed.

Very gently, he turned the handle. I could hardly hear it, but felt it swing open.

Not a sound in the darkness.

He crouched, flashed a beam down the passage. Nothing. Silence.

He stepped through and I followed, my hand touching the wall. A floorboard creaked and we stopped. Moved on.

Complete silence. Faint light from an open door. Jones's shadow. My fingers on the wall. A piece of plaster crunched and we stopped again.

Silence. Almost there. I touched his shoulder. He turned, touched my arm. I saw his hand find the knob. The door opened, silhouetting him. He went inside.

We've missed him, I thought dully, we'll never catch him now.

Light sprang from the torch–

'Christ!'

Footsteps crossed the room.

After a moment he said, 'You'd better come in, Chris.'

I stepped inside. Jones stood beside the bed and in the light from his torch, John's face stared back at me.

I don't know how I knew it was John. His face was black, cheeks puffed out like a balloon. Eyes like screwed-up paper. Thickened lips drawn back over still perfect teeth. And the smell.

But it was John.

CHAPTER 18

Jones pocketed his gun. 'Hold this for me, will you?' He handed me the torch and began methodically to search John's pockets. The smell surrounded us.

'Ah.' Jones pulled something from the breast pocket. 'Let's have some light … a library ticket… Mr John Devlin.' He looked up. 'We need more than that, really.'

I swallowed. 'He used to wear a pendant round his neck, a thistle…'

Jones said resignedly, 'Shine the torch.' He compressed his lips and undid the shirt buttons. Picked something up with two fingers. 'That it?'

I nodded, unable to speak.

His head jerked up. 'Put it out, quick!' As he moved over to the window, I heard a car approach. Its lights momentarily lit the room.

'Range-Rover,' said Jones softly, peering from the side. 'What's the betting it was the one by the river?'

A faint squeal of brakes, then the engine

died. A door opened and clicked shut.

'Who is it?'

'I can't see from here, but they're coming in. Come on.'

I followed him back into the corridor and the next room. He pulled me behind the door.

'We left everything as we found it, didn't we?' he muttered. 'Lab keys, tapes, the door up here...' He took out his gun. 'Don't do anything, we must catch him with the body–'

The door at the end of the corridor opened and Jones gripped my arm. Footsteps on the wooden boards, the bobbing light of a torch through the crack ... the shadow as he moved past. Jones still held my arm. The smell seemed to cling to him.

Silence. More footsteps, then a gurgling noise that I couldn't place. Nor could Jones at first. Then, as it stopped–

'Oh bloody hell!' He ran out into the corridor. 'Hold it! Don't–'

I followed. There was a whoosh as the petrol ignited and a tall figure jumped out in front of us.

'Hold it!' shouted Jones again, levelling the gun at him.

The figure turned, faced us for an instant. I snapped on the torch, not that it was necessary – I had already recognized his profile against the flames.

Charles Hampton.

He gave a strangled cry, dropped the can he was holding and ran down the corridor.

'Stop, or I'll shoot!'

He took no notice and Jones fired a shot over his head. It made no difference.

Jones turned to me. 'Can he get out that way?'

'I don't think so.'

'Right.' He started running.

I followed, but something made me pause and look into John's room. The bed was a funeral pyre, the flames curling round the dark shape of his body.

'Bring that bloody torch!' shouted Jones, and I ran after him.

At the far end of the corridor Charles was struggling with a door. He turned, flung his own torch at Jones and darted into the last of the rooms. The door slammed.

Jones reached it and tried the handle.

'He's locked it!' he said as I reached him. He turned back to the door. 'Hampton!' he shouted. 'You'd better come out or you'll be trapped.'

No answer.

'We're not going to hurt you. Better give

yourself up than be burned.'

Still nothing.

Jones looked back down the corridor. Already, the flames were licking the ceiling.

'We'd better get out and raise the alarm,' he said. 'He's not worth risking patients' lives for.'

'You go, I'm staying–'

'Don't be a fool.'

'I need him – alive.'

'You've already got all the evidence you need to–'

'I'm handing him over, alive. Give me the gun, then go and raise the alarm. Get some people to hold a blanket under the window–'

'You're coming with me.'

I smiled and shook my head.

He looked at me and realized I meant it, then looked past me to where the fire had taken hold of the corridor.

He pressed the gun into my hand, said, 'Good luck,' then started running back. He paused in front of the flames and tore off his jacket, covered his head with it and leapt…

For an instant he was etched, black against yellow, then as he disappeared, part of the ceiling fell in a shower of sparks.

I ran up the corridor. 'Tom! Are you all right?'

No answer. A vortex of flame licked me, singed my hair, and I fell back.

Back at the door, I yelled, 'Charles, it's me, Chris Randall. I'm coming in.'

Thinking: Well, it works on television, I aimed the gun at the lock. The recoil surprised me. I fired three more times, then kicked at the door. It flew open the second time.

He was standing by the window, motionless, looking out.

'Charles.'

He didn't move. I approached him.

'Charles!'

Still no movement.

'Jones has gone for help. He won't be long.'

'Jones, I suppose, is Dave.' He didn't look round.

'Yes.'

Now he turned. Saw the gun in my hand.

'Why don't you shoot me? You can say it was self-defence.'

'I need you alive.'

'I don't.'

He lunged at me, at the gun, his strength overwhelming me. I fired into the floor, kept firing until there were just clicks, then let him take it. He stared at it in his hands.

I went to the door and looked up the corridor. The fire had spread to another room.

I closed the door and wedged it with a piece of wood. Charles was still staring at the gun. He slowly raised his head.

'Why did you do that?'

'I told you, I need you alive.'

'And I told you, I don't want to live.'

Something in his voice brought the rage boiling to my head and I strode over to him.

'It isn't going to be that easy for you, Charles,' I said between my teeth. 'You're going to *live,* you're going to tell the police what you did and after that you're going to prison.' My chest heaved. 'You're not going to like prison, Charles. I know. I've been there.'

He stared back at me.

'Why did you do it, Charles?'

Still he stared.

'I said, why? Why?' I screamed, kicking his legs. '*Why, why, why?*' I drove my fists into his belly, his face. He stood there, not moving, just silently accepting everything I did to him.

'Why, Charles?' I said, pleading with him now.

'I don't know.'

'Please tell me.'

His lips moved. He turned to the window again, then started speaking in a low voice, barely audible at first.

'I don't know. I'm not a snob, you know, I can't help the way I speak any more than ... than he could. I didn't hate him either, not to begin with. We were working together at Parc-Reed. Except that John – Mr John Stuart Devlin – he wouldn't work *with* anyone.

'We were supposed to be investigating the molecular structure of HIV. I tried, I really tried, but he just ... wouldn't ... stop. He had to make me look small at every opportunity. I tried to build bridges. I invited him to my home, and d'you know what he did?' He turned a ravaged face to me. *'He seduced my wife.'*

He looked away. 'Our marriage was already shaky, but that finished it. When I found out, I hated him more than anything, more than the Devil. I went into work ... we had a fight. We were carpeted. When it all came out, he was sacked, and I was put on the road. As a *"Products Specialist"*.' He infused the words with a bottomless contempt.

'Sarah left me. I tried to pick up my life. I'm a scientist. I thought: If I work, do as

261

I'm told for a while, they'll let me back into the laboratory.

'I worked. Hard. Then I was sent to Oxford National Microbiology Lab to help them instal the new Parc-Reed anti-HIV test. John was there. I don't know why I stayed any longer than I had to, morbid curiosity, I suppose. Then Peter Carey, with whom I got on, suggested I stay for a while and look at ways of improving their other techniques.

'Of course, Parc-Reed leapt at it, told me to stay as long as Peter wanted me. So I did, and before long I guessed what John was doing. Then, I *had* to stay.' His eyes twisted round to me. 'You see, it was my idea in the first place, looking at the regulatory proteins of HIV. I remember mentioning it to him in the early days. *My* idea.'

I didn't believe him. I could see in his face it was something he'd convinced himself of.

'And he was going to sell it to America for a fortune. My idea. Or Parc-Reed's, or Great Britain's, whichever you like, he was going to sell it, sell us all, and not even for greed. It was to spite us, because of the chip on his shoulder.

'Anyway, at the Christmas Party, Peter got the scent of it, which is why he didn't sack

John. Peter needed to get his name on some original work, which is why he wanted people like John and me around him. He spoke to me afterwards, asked whether I knew what John was doing. I told him what I guessed. Then he suggested, obliquely, that I find out more, so that he could get rid of John and he and I work on it.'

He smiled wryly. 'I gave him an equally oblique reply, then went straight to my old Head of Department at Parc-Reed, who thanked me and said leave it with him.

'I asked a month later what was happening.'

Before my eyes, Charles's face grew old and hunted. 'I was told to mind my own business and get on with the job I was paid for. I realized then that nothing was happening.' He raised his eyes to me. 'But I was wrong, wasn't I?'

'Yes,' I said, 'Tom Jones was sent to look into it.'

'If only I'd known.' He stared out of the window again. I could smell smoke, but didn't dare to stop him talking.

'That night,' he said, 'that Friday before you came back, I decided to have it out with him. Everyone else had gone. I went to his lab and told him what I knew. He laughed at me. He was even more bloody than usual. I don't know why.'

I did, of course; it would have been just after his row with Tom Jones.

Charles's voice started trembling.

'I kept my temper somehow and told him that he and I should hand the work back to Parc-Reed. I even offered to try and get his job back. D'you know what he did? He told me I couldn't even handle a woman, let alone a scientific concept.

'*Then he started telling me how he'd seduced Sarah.* I told him to stop or I'd kill him. "I'll kill you," I said. He just laughed. He didn't stop. I couldn't see anything. I lashed out. And then when I could see, he was on the floor, dead...'

'You're sure he was dead?'

'Oh yes. I do know how to use my hands.' He shuddered. 'I was going to ring 999, really I was, my hand was on the 'phone, but then I thought: Why should I? He had it coming to him. I'll dump the body later and no one will know.

'I was looking for somewhere to hide him temporarily when I found the room up here. I put him in a cupboard and shut the door...'

'What about his shoes?' I said urgently.

'Oh yes, his shoes … they fell off when I dragged him into the room. I meant to put them into the cupboard after him, but I forgot.

'Then I went to Greece, after I'd seen you that Monday. At first I was just numb, but then I thought: It was an accident, I can't bring him back. Why let his data go to waste? Why not hand that back to Parc-Reed? I knew it was in the computer, so I caught a plane on Saturday and came up here late that evening. I … searched him and found his keys. I saw his shoes as I was going, but I couldn't bear to look at him again so I took them with me.'

There was so much I wanted to ask, but I didn't dare interrupt the flow, now that he was approaching the critical part of his story.

'I thought the best time to search his flat would be Sunday morning. I knew there had to be a password, you see. I drove round, the shoes were still in my car, so I took them up. I'd been there half an hour, maybe more, when I heard Sally.'

He swallowed and closed his eyes. The smoke was thicker now, and I could hear the fire raging beyond the wall.

'Go on,' I said.

'I – I hid in the kitchen behind the door. Heard her rummaging around, then she 'phoned you. There was no way out of the kitchen. Oh God! If I'd only stunned her before she'd seen me...'

Sirens wailed in the distance. People were rushing around outside in the light cast by the flames.

'Go on!' I said urgently.

'She came in, put the kettle on, she was humming to herself, then she turned and saw me. I – I told her John had something of mine, I was just looking for it... I thought for a moment I'd convinced her, but then she saw his keys on the worktop...

'She picked them up, then looked at me and said, "You've killed him, haven't you..."

'She got past me somehow, and made it to the bedroom door before I caught her ... then she was on the floor, I don't even remember hitting her but I knew she was dead, I carried her over to the bed, then you came up, I hadn't even shut the door–' He cut off abruptly, then started again.

'I'm sorry. You just stared at her, I hit you hard enough to stun you, then dialled 999 and left the receiver... I was on my way out, then I pulled off her jeans to make it look like a sex attack... I'm so sorry, Chris, I beg your pardon...'

'How did you get out?'

'Oh, down the stairs and through a window into the back garden. I went back to my London flat and stayed there until it was time to return to Oxford. When I heard about your escape, I knew you'd come back. I tried to find an excuse to stay away, but the firm insisted I remain here. It was all ordained. I had no choice but to sit here and wait for you.' He turned to me. 'I'm glad now that–'

The door behind us burst into flames. I looked out of the window. A group of people outside were holding a blanket. I found a piece of wood and was about to smash the glass when Charles shouted.

'No! Sharp edges, better open it!'

We both stood under it and heaved. It wouldn't move. My back grew hotter.

'Harder!' shouted Charles.

I thought my arms would crack, then it shifted. I pushed it up.

'You first,' I said, turning to him, only then seeing his hand chopping sideways at me.

I remember the blow, sinking, being caught up, a sensation of floating, then nothing.

CHAPTER 19

'Can you hear me?'

I opened my eyes. A ring of faces hung over me.

'How do you feel?'

'OK … I think.'

I felt awful. I felt as though I'd been away for years in some other dream-life where everything was fine until I'd been dragged back here. I found out later I'd been unconscious for about five minutes.

Professional hands deftly searched my body, then my head.

'Nothing broken, might be some concussion, though. Better get him over to Swindon with the rest.' The doctor excused himself and hurried away.

The noises, which had been just a background until then, suddenly grew louder and for a moment I thought I must be in a fairground. Wailing sirens, engines rumbling, people shouting.

I raised myself to my elbows.

There were people everywhere. The lines

of third- and fourth-storey windows along the wing glowed as though someone had turned all the lights on. Flames pushed their way through one or two.

The hospital was being evacuated, a stream of stretcher-bearers poured from the main block to a waiting fleet of ambulances. More shouts as another fire engine drew up beside the two already there in a medley of horns and lights–

Charles!

I looked over to the window from where he'd thrown me: it was belching smoke and fire.

Ignoring the people around me, I struggled to my feet and looked round for Jones. The firemen were starting to run hoses over to the burning wing. I couldn't see him. A police car drew up and the familiar sickness of fear took me...

'Chris?' It was Jones.

I griped his arm. 'Charles, is he...?'

He slowly shook his head. 'It doesn't matter. We've still got enough to clear you. Did he tell you anything?'

'Everything. How he killed John ... and then Sally.'

'Good, it'll help. Chris, you're going to have to trust me now.'

I knew instantly what he meant. 'I'm not going to be locked up again?'

'It'll only be for a day, maybe two. I'll come with–'

'No!' I tried to break away from him but he was holding my arm.

'If you run, they'll catch you and it'll make it worse.'

I stood there panting, realizing the truth of his words. Then I let him lead me to the police car.

I thought my reason would leave me when they clamped the cuff to my wrist, but as we left the city, I became calmer.

Tom Jones was going to clear me. I'd pick up a sort of life. The other dream-life was real and Jill and Sally were in it. It was going to be all right.

As we took the Swindon exit from the roundabout, I had one last glimpse of the city: spires, towers and domes silhouetted in the ruddy glow of the still burning hospital.

The city of Dreaming Spires. A bed of nails. It depends on your point of view.

The publishers hope that this book has given you enjoyable reading. Large Print Books are especially designed to be as easy to see and hold as possible. If you wish a complete list of our books please ask at your local library or write directly to:

Dales Large Print Books
Magna House, Long Preston,
Skipton, North Yorkshire.
BD23 4ND

This Large Print Book, for people
who cannot read normal print,
is published under the auspices of

THE ULVERSCROFT FOUNDATION